Christmas Eve on Hwy 41

By Edward J Funk

Table of Contents

Chapter 1: Christmas Eve 1955

Mother and son are both in the large open area that runs across the front of the old farm house. The expanse is comprised of the living room, an alcove west of the living room, and the dining room. The mother's name is Mary. At forty-eight year's old, she's an attractive woman in a sensible kind of way. She's wearing a sensible housedress and low heel shoes that lace up the front. She has dark hair, dark eyes, and is seemingly unconcerned with the twenty pounds she's gained in her seventeen years of marriage.

The son, Joseph, is 10. He is surprisingly average in appearance, considering how much he looks like his handsome father. His height and weight are average. Where he's not average is his hyper sensitivity, as well as his ability to absorb everything going on around him. The first aspect probably begets the second.

Joseph is the youngest of the four children. The three oldest are with their dad in New York for their aunt's funeral.

The wind is howling and a blizzard has kicked up. A fir Christmas tree occupies most of the alcove. There are loads of presents underneath the bottom branches, but Joseph manages to scoot around to look out of a south facing window.

He observes, "The wind sounds like it's coming from all directions."

His mother, who has been paying bills on the dining room table, replies, "It does sound like that but it's coming from the east. It's so forceful that it's swirling all around the house."

Joseph laments, "A good blizzard being wasted during Christmas vacation. When I think of all the times I've looked out this window hoping not to see the school bus, then the red light starts blinking in the distance. Just isn't fair. On top of that, it's a Saturday, so I'd still be out of school anyway. Just isn't fair."

Joseph's mind slips into another gear and says, "You know when I was in New York last summer with Dad and Grandpa...when Grandpa wasn't looking...Aunt Kathleen would sneak a cigarette. Do you think that the cigarette smoking had anything to do with her dying?"

Mary replies, "No. Kathleen died from kidney disease."

"How could it happen so suddenly?"

Mary answers, "I don't know."

Joseph turns on the TV but static commands all four channels. He turns it off again and starts roaming aimlessly. As he's passing through the breakfast room the phone rings. Joseph answers.

Bernard, his dad, is calling from a phone booth at LaGuardia airport.

Joseph says, "Hello."

"It's Dad, Joseph. I'm at the airport in New York."

Joseph is thrilled to be talking on such a long distance phone call. He asks, "When will you guys be home?"

"That's why I'm calling. All the flights into Chicago are cancelled."

"So when will you be home?"

"I don't know yet."

"Did Kathleen's little kids go to the funeral?"

Mary approaches and says, "Give me the phone. You can ask all the questions you want when he gets home. This is an expensive call."

Speaking to her husband, she inquires, "Where are you?

"We're at La Guardia but all the flights are cancelled into Midway (Chicago airport.) I just called Cletus (Bernard's cousin who lives in Manhasset, Long Island) before calling you. He has invited us to return to his house to stay until we can get out."

"You wouldn't have been able to get home anyway. We're in the midst of a blizzard. It's probably this same storm that has Midway closed."

"I don't like the idea of you and Joseph being there by yourselves. Call Dick (a neighbor and good friend on the farm just north) and let him know you and Joseph are home alone. That way he'll know to check to see you're alright."

"We'll be fine, but I'll call Dick right after we hang up."

Just as Mary is hanging up, there is a large crashing sound. Thinking it was a tree in the front yard, Joseph goes to a dining room window to look. Mary picks up the phone again to call the neighbor; the phone is dead.

Chapter 2: Visitors of the Moneyed Class

A telephone pole south of the house landed across both lanes of the road. It just missed crashing onto a car travelling in the northbound lane. The car is a 1955 Cadillac, two toned, dark blue top and sky-blue bottom. The license plate begins with AA, an indication that the car is registered in Marion County, location of Indiana's capitol city, Indianapolis.

The couple inside, both in their mid-forties, are Jack and Helen Cooper. Jack's in the driver's seat. He's wearing a sweater and slacks; his camel haired coat's in the back seat. Helen is wearing a blonde mink coat over a chocolate brown maternity outfit and fur-lined boots. Both have held onto their collegiate good looks, but the tightness in Jack's face and the fatigue in Helen's have diminished the effortless quality that had previously been present. Jack has a reddish blonde flattop and Helen's mid-length hair is now blonder than in her college days. It has been cared for by the same beautician at Ayres Department store for the past five years.

Jack exclaims in a loud voice, "My God! That could have hit us. And for God's sake, we're now in the ditch. The drifting snow can just go ahead and finish the job of burying us!" His voice now even louder, "And here you are, expecting a baby in three weeks, a baby we've waited twenty-two-years for, and we're stuck in the Goddamn wilderness."

Helen, going into the familiar attempt to downshift Jack's mood, voices soothingly, "Honey, we're okay. I'm okay. You're okay. And the baby's okay." She continues, "I see what looks like a large house on this side of the road. I don't think it's more than 50 yards away."

Jack attempts to look and then says, "I hadn't planned on spending Christmas Eve with some farm yokels. The more I think about it, this just seems to be getting worse."

Helen thinks to herself, "We wouldn't be in this ditch if you weren't hell-bent to attend a Christmas Eve party with an old fraternity buddy. And of course it's all about landing a new account for your advertising agency."

She says, "Let go up to that house."

"In your condition, I don't think you should be walking through snow drifts."

"Jack, I think I'm a better judge of what I can and cannot do."

"I'm not so sure. Let me carry you. I'd feel a lot more confident."

Helen cautions, "With your bad back?"

"I'll carry you and that's final."

"Let's get going then."

"If we need our luggage later on I'll come back for it."

With the phone dead, it is apparent to Mary and Joseph that the crashing sound and the dead phone are related. They both go to the windows facing south. They notice a car in the ditch just south of where the fallen pole crosses the road. Mary tells Joseph to put his coat and boots on and then go ask the people to come up to the house. But before Joseph gets out the door, Mary sees people getting out of the car. She calls, "Joseph, you don't need to go; they're on their way."

Mary goes back to the dining room to clear off the table. Joseph goes back to the window. Mary asks, "How many people are there?"

"I think one is carrying another. Yeah, it's just two."

Mary discerns there is enough time to give each of the bathrooms "a lick and a promise." That's an expression she uses when giving a room the minimal attention needed to be presentable. And while she's in the upstairs bathroom, she "puts on her face," meaning applying makeup. Today, that only means powder and lipstick.

The front door enters into a small rectangular hall. From there, French doors offer entries to both the living room and the dining room. The front door is seldom used; people in a farming community usually come to the back door. These are strangers so Joseph is expecting them at the front door. Mary returns from upstairs and is right behind him.

They knock and Joseph opens the door. Mary says, "Hello! Welcome!"

Jack is all smiles and is in his "You're going to love me" mode that has worked so well with clients over the years. He shakes Mary's hand. "You don't know how relieved we are that your home was nearby. A telephone pole went down right in front of us and we skidded off into the ditch."

Helen is also smiling. She utters, "Yes, I think we're pretty fortunate considering what could have happened."

Mary states, "My name is Mary, Mary Brow. This is my son, Joseph. 'Joseph, take their coats and hang them on the back hooks; they can drip off the snow to their heart's content.' I'm sorry that I can't offer you the phone. It went out when the pole came down."

Jack pronounces, "We're the Coopers. Please call us Jack and Helen."

Mary suggests, "Helen, you can take your boots off right here. Joseph, after you hang the coats up, go upstairs and get a pair of your father's wool socks for both Mr. and Mrs. Cooper."

They hand their coats to Joseph. He likes the feel of Helen's mink coat and knows it means money. When his parents let him stay up late on Friday night to watch an old movie, models for Chicago-based Eden's Furs promote such extravagant wares. And looking at Mrs. Cooper, Joseph thinks she even looks like one of those models, except none of them are pregnant.

The whole idea of "pregnant" has taken on new meaning to Joseph in that he had just recently become aware of the facts-of-life. He had grasped since before starting school that a baby comes from the mom's stomach. He had seen that often enough from noticing women in church before a new baby is born. But a few months earlier, his mom gave him a book to read about how babies are made. The book was really written as a guide to help a parent explain the facts-of-life to their child, but his mom decided the simplest thing to do was let him read it for himself.

What Joseph didn't grasp from reading that book was the pleasure the parents derived from the sexual act. Instead, he concluded that a man and a woman were willing to go through laborious calisthenics just to have a baby. Joseph thought that quite noble of them. Joseph brings that same upright thought to the Coopers. Then his mind turned to the question, "Where are you coming from?"

Jack answers, "We're coming from Indianapolis, young man. Have you ever had the chance to visit our state capitol?"

Joseph gives him an ill-mannered look and replies, "Yeah, lots of times, more times than I can count."

Mary looks at Joseph and gives a negative shake of her head to let her son know he was out of line. Jack has a look of disquiet on his face, but then Mary explains, "Indianapolis was my home before I married and came up here. This is where my husband's business is situated." Mary continues, "We make frequent trips to Indianapolis to visit my family."

Joseph had already turned on the Christmas lights for the inside tree but while he is still in the entry way, he plugs in the cord for the outside lights. As he does, he says, "I don't know why I'm doing this if no one is going to be driving by."

Helen comments, "Turning those lights on means you have a romantic soul." Joseph isn't sure what this means...but he likes the sound of it.

Then Helen turns toward Mary and says, "Thank you for being so gracious, total strangers barging in on Christmas Eve!"

Mary smiles and replies, "Please, come into the living room where you'll be more comfortable."

The walls of the living room are a soft cream-colored plaster with wavy texturing. The carpet is of a maroon colored pattern and the furniture, a plush deep blue. The draperies pick up these exact colors in a floral pattern. Crystals drip from the wall sconces, which match the crystals hanging from the chandelier in the dining room. There is an oil painting of a man in a blue suit hanging above the sofa. There's also a fruit bowl watercolor over the piano. In the southeast corner, on top of a blonde hi/fi set, a stable and Nativity figures are displayed.

Helen and Jack both sit down on the sofa. Jack's descent makes obvious his back problem. Helen's not surprised; he had insisted on carrying her.

She looks around the room and wonders if a decorator was involved. Jack's made similar observations but they only tell him that money's been spent. Turning and looking at the portrait of the man he asks, "Is that your husband?"

Mary affirms, "Yes. He just called before the phone went out. He and our older children are stranded in New York."

Jack wonders, "What's a farm family doing in New York?"

Resisting the urge to ask, he instead pivots to his need to control and asserts, "As I'm sure you've noticed, Helen is expecting. We need to take good care of her."

Mary smiles in reply and then asks, "What can I offer to warm you? I can open a can of soup or make some coffee. Or would you rather have tea?"

Helen responds, "Coffee sounds wonderful." Jack concurs. Mary leaves the room.

Helen telegraphs a look to Jack that says, "You're not in charge here," but then she smiles at him and says, "Honey, settle down."

"I just had a terrifying thought. What if the baby decides to come early and we're stuck in God-forsaken nowhere."

"Honey, do you think I'd agree to come on this trip if I thought there was a chance of that happening?"

"I'm just uncomfortable being stuck here. And, who are these people? What are they doing living here?"

Helen states, "Who is being provincial? You think anyone living in the country should be gathering eggs in the hen house. That they never go anywhere. That they've never been anywhere."

"Even if it isn't true in this house, it's probably true for most country homes."

"Don't be so sure." She moves over and grabs Jack's hand, "Let me tell you what I really want for Christmas."

"I thought I already knew."

"But now it's something else. I want to roll the clock back twenty-two years and rediscover the people we were, but put us in this house at this time. I want us to see this situation, stranded at an old farm house on a Christmas Eve, as a romantic adventure."

"What's gotten into you? We're in our forties, not our twenties. We can't pretend otherwise. Look. I'll do my best to do my best."

"And this from a man who runs the largest advertising agency in Indianapolis. Jack, you sell fantasy. Can't you bite off a piece of it for yourself?"

Jack retorts, "I sell myself. The creative people sell the fantasy." He manages a smile, but adds, "Helen, you know I can only be who I am. No one knows that better than you."

Helen returns his smile and says, "I do. And obviously, you don't know how you change from one moment to the next." She pats Jack's hand signifying that the conversation has come to a close.

A few minutes later, Mary brings in coffee. Realizing that Jack and Helen must be curious, she explains, "My husband, Bernard and our three oldest children are in in New York for a sad occasion. His youngest sister died quite suddenly from kidney disease. The funeral was this morning. Now Midway is closed because of the storm and they can't get out of New York. These roads will be closed as well, if they're not already, so he wouldn't have been able to get home tonight anyway."

Meanwhile, a second car is stalled behind the Coopers.

Chapter 3: Runaways

The car is a 1950 dark green Chevrolet. The occupants are a young couple, Keith, age 19, and Sandy, age 16. Keith has brown curly hair and brown eyes. His build is small and wiry and his face, despite the fact that he has never really known childhood, still looks childish. He's wearing jeans and an obviously faux leather jacket, torn at the left elbow. Sandy is wearing a tired looking gray wool coat. Her hair, in a ponytail, is dish-water blonde. Another girl with the same features might mistakenly think she looks like Debbie Reynolds, but Sandy has few allusions. Her family life has been chaos. She's the most stable person in it. Keith has convinced her to run away, and the car they're using belongs to her stepfather.

Joseph has returned to the alcove window and observes, "Mom, it looks like another car is stuck behind the Cooper's. They still have their headlights on."

Mary joins him at the window. She says to her son, "Put your coat and boots on and go out and invite them in."

In the green Chevrolet, Sandy, a city girl, feels intimidated by what appears to be endless open space. She exclaims, "Keith, I'm scared. Maybe the pole across the road is a sign telling us to turn around and go back home. I can face whatever we have to face."

Keith declares, "Maybe you can. You're not the one who "borrowed" Larry's car. My ass will be in jail within an hour. Besides, I don't think we can turn around. Too much snow. Just hold tight, the phone company's got to know something's happened out here."

Doubtfully, Sandy replies, I'm not seeing anybody coming from the other direction either. Oh, Keith, we're stranded in this blizzard. It's just going to get worse."

"Just don't panic. That won't help anything."

"I'm just noticing, there doesn't appear to be anyone in that car in front of us. There must be a house nearby."

Keith spots Joseph and says, "Someone's coming."

Sandy reacts, "Oh, thank God."

Keith, counters, "It looks like a kid. Let me do the talking."

Joseph trudges to the driver's side window. Keith rolls it down halfway.

Joseph says, "My mom wants you to come up to the house. You'll be nice and warm until the road opens again."

"Thank your mom for us. But we have plenty of gas to keep the car going and we'd just as soon stay here."

Joseph is lost for words. He wasn't expecting this reaction.

Keith repeats, "Tell your mom thanks just the same." He rolls the window back up.

Sandy asserts, "I'm going with him," and reaches for the door. Keith grabs her left hand to hold her in. Sandy tries yanking away and yells, "Let go of me."

Joseph, who had turned toward the house, hears Sandy shouting. He turns back and is looking at the two of them. Keith realizes that the kid's watching them and knows he has to let go. He says, "Okay, okay. We'll go with the little bastard but put that ring on your finger I gave you this morning."

Sandy declares, "You know I don't like you using a word like that," but she reaches into her pocket and pulls out the ring. As Sandy and Keith both get out of the car, Keith says to Joseph, "On second thought, we'll come with you. It's sure real nice of your mom to invite us in."

When the three reached the house, Joseph takes them to the back door. Mainly, it's just his habit. But he also knows that his mother would want them to hang their coats on the back hooks situated above the landing leading to the basement.

Mary hears them come in, and is now at the back of the house to greet them. "Come in! Come in! Hang up your coats. My name is Mary Brow and you've met Joseph."

They really didn't know the boy's name but they nodded their heads in affirmation. A few awkward seconds pass before Sandy replies, "My name is Sandy; he's Keith."

Keith looks uncomfortable but then he grabs Sandy's hand with the ring on it, holds it up, and avows, "Yeah, she's my wife."

This forced gesture generates quick flecks of discomfort on the faces of Mary and Sandy.

Mary replies invitingly, "Come into the living room and meet the Coopers. They're our guests as well, compliments of the fallen pole."

As they're walking into the living room, Keith takes the initiative and announces, "I'm Keith Logan and this is my wife Sandy."

 Keith is wearing a horizontal blue and white striped cotton shirt and jeans. Sandy is wearing a white blouse and a full beige corduroy skirt. Their attire accentuates their obvious youth. Jack struggles to stand up and says, "I'm Jack Cooper and this is my wife Helen."

Keith had made up the name Logan. That ruse, along with the claim of being married, has made him cocky with the success of his deceptions. He replies to the Coopers, "Real nice to meet you."

Sandy's facial affect is flat but she manages a slight smile toward the Coopers. Both she and Keith sit down. He in a rocking chair, she in an individual chair covered in the same blue plush as the sofa.

Mary breaks the silence by saying, "There's a story behind that rocker. My parents were Irish immigrants who met is this country. They were poor but somehow managed to get...I'll never understand how this happened...seventeen rocking chairs for wedding presents. This is the one they kept. The others they returned and bought stoves to heat the house."

Jack utters, "There must have been some unbelievable sale on rocking chairs that week!"

Mary responds, "That's the story my parents told me. Pop might have enhanced the number; he was a wonderful story teller. But my mother wouldn't have. Life has always been a serious affair for her."

Jack inquires, "What business was your father in?"

"He and Mom ran a corner grocery. Mom really ran the business. Dad was the butcher who chatted with the customers who were also our neighbors. In those days, most people didn't own cars, so their purchases were limited to what they could carry home. That meant they'd shopped every day or two."

Curious, Jack asks, "Where was their grocery store?"

"On the corner of New York and Rural."

Sandy, who had only been half listening, now asks, "New York and Rural in Indianapolis?"

Mary responds, "Yes. Does that mean that you're from Indianapolis as well?"

Sandy affirms, "Yes."

Jack chimes in, "So are we," but he doesn't ask where in Indianapolis Sandy and Keith live. He knows it wouldn't be anyway near his home on Washington Boulevard.

The apparent reality that everyone knows all about Indianapolis perturbs Keith. He no longer feels as free to spin any narrative that comes into his mind. His uneasiness spills into the room.

Chapter 4: Moving into Action

The spell is soon broken by the hissing and pops of the steam radiators, and these sounds compete with the howls of the gusting winds. It prompts Jack to ask Mary, "How is this house heated? Coal or Oil?"

Mary replies, "Coal. We're going to convert to oil but that will be a summer project."

Jack asks, "Would you like me to keep an eye on the furnace? Growing up, my family ran a heating/cooling business and I worked there during my summer vacations."

"Yes, I'd appreciate that."

Helen rejoins, "Jack, please try not to aggravate your back."

Mary offers, "If the stoker needs coal, Joseph can help with that."

Keith, sensing a chance at inclusion, abandons his hitherto manipulative calculations, and says in a sincere voice, "Let me help; I'd really like to."

Keith barely remembers the house he lived in with his mom and dad. After his dad took off, they lived with his grandmother for a few years. Then it was a series of apartments, all situated in a neighborhood that continued to slip further downhill. It would be a brand new experience for Keith to keep a furnace going.

Jack and Keith walk to the back of the house with Joseph leading the way. Once the men are in the basement, Joseph claims a familiar perch on a linoleum-covered step. It was from here that he has watched his dad tend the furnace on so many winter nights. Now the ritual is being performed by two strangers.

Jack spots the claw-like-grips hanging on the wall used to remove the cinders from the furnace. He asks Joseph, "Where does your dad put these cinders once he removes them from the furnace?"

"There's an old metal bushel basket. It's under the steps."

Jack says to Keith, "Use the gloves hanging there and open the furnace door."

Keith complies and a blast of hot air comes out.

Jack explains, "Notice that some clunks are fiery red and some are gray. The fiery ones still have organic matter burning and that's where the heat is coming from. The gray clunks have passed that stage and are cinders. They need to come out to make room for more coal to burn. Use these grips to extract the cinders and put them is the metal basket."

Joseph loves gazing into the furnace when the door is open. Watching the flames of red and orange dashing from the coals has always made him feel secure. Not just that he'd be kept warm in the old house but that he had a dad who always saw to it. Thinking of his dad, he says, "My dad told me that's energy from the sun's in there. That's where the energy originally came from. Where all energy comes from."

Jack confirms, "Your dad's right, Joseph."

Keith is listening. He has no idea of what they're talking about.

The half-filled metal bushel basket remains near the furnace. Jack says to Keith, "Now it's time to put fresh coal into the stoker. Sorry you're the one who has to do all the work but I aggravated an already sore back coming to the house from our car. So, grab that shovel hanging on the wall, scoop some coal from the coal room, and dump it in the stoker."

Without consciously being aware, Joseph loves this part of the ritual. Scooping the coal and dumping it into the stoker triggered a rich aroma, millions of years in the making.

Keith brings several scoopfuls to the stoker. As he's bringing another, Jack signals to Keith that this will be the last one for now. Keith hangs the shovel back on the wall hook.

Jack asks, "Joseph what does your dad do with the old cinders?"

Looking toward Keith, Joseph says, "It will probably be easier if I show you."

Jack walks up the stairs and goes to the front of the house. Keith grabs the bushel basket and follows Joseph. Neither bother to put on their coats.

The gravel driveway, drifting with snow, consists of a lane coming up from the highway and then opening to a circle. The entry to the barnyard (although there's no longer a barn) is just opposite of the lane. This is where Joseph directs Keith to dump the cinders. They silently return to the house.

By now, Mary and Helen are in the kitchen having a second cup of coffee. Joseph and Keith return the metal bushel basket to the basement and then pass through the kitchen to the front part of the house.

Helen inquires, "You mentioned your three oldest children. How old are they?"

"Tom is sixteen, Carol is fifteen, and Ann is fourteen. They're all in high school, all attending boarding schools. Their Christmas vacation started earlier than Joseph's, so they were able to go with their dad."

Looking around, Helen comments, "This looks like a brand new kitchen."

Mary confirms, "Practically. It was redone a year ago last summer. The original house, built in the 1880s, stopped right there." She points to the wall separating the kitchen from the adjoining room and adds, "We now call the original kitchen the breakfast room. It's very handy space because it provides the added cupboards and drawers. And, sometimes, if it's just Joseph and me, we'll eat at that little table. I don't know how old that table is; it came with the house."

Helen asks, "Did you add this whole wing?"

Mary responds, "I'm confusing the situation. This wing was added in the late thirties, a few years before we moved in. So what we recently remodeled was the 1930s kitchen."

"It's quite lovely. I love the widows. It must be interesting looking through them all year long. You must be more aware of the change of seasons than we are in the city."

"Interesting that you say that. I do enjoy looking out at the lawn and the fields as they change throughout the year. Being a city girl, this was a whole new experience, a very different way of living."

"I hope you don't mind me being so inquisitive. How did you get from your parent's grocery store to here?"

"During the Depression I couldn't find a job. So my great aunt Mary put me through college. She had worked in the Theodore Roosevelt home in Oyster Bay, New York, as a seamstress and had saved her money. That's how families took care of each other during the Depression, particularly immigrant families like mine. I'm telling you way more than what you asked….."

"No, please. I'd love to hear the story."

"I graduated from Indiana University and became a social worker. I was perfectly content with being a career woman and the years passed. My mother wasn't as content. She thought I should be looking for a husband. We're Catholic. There was a novena service at our parish church, which meant going to church nine evenings in a row. To placate my mother, I agreed to attend with the intention of seeking guidance. As it turned out, on the last evening, Bernard approached me and asked if he could walk me home. I said yes."

Helen states, "I assumed that he was from here and that's why you moved up here."

"Yes, he did grow up in this community. But he worked a few years in Indianapolis and during that time he played tennis with my sister. That's how I met him."

Helen replies in an upbeat voice, "So he was the answer to your prayers. How romantic."

Mary responds, "It sounds that way, doesn't it?" Helen thought she detected a tone in Mary's voice that was less than convincing. It left her wondering.

Mary continues, "My husband and his brothers have a hybrid seed corn business and their operating plant is in Kentland, the town just north of here. They're in the business of genetics so they offer farmers seeds that promise higher yields. The business is both genetics and marketing. And, the "why here" is because this farm serves as the nursery where those hybrids are bred. They wanted a location on the highway that would help promote their business. Your car ran off the road just beyond a large sign with a big ear of corn on it, the background of their company logo."

"I didn't notice it; the blowing snow was such a distraction. But once we swerved off the road, I did notice your home. Thank God! And now that I'm inside, it's certainly a beautiful home."

Mary replies, "I've grown to love it."

Mary isn't telling Helen the whole story. Nor would it be appropriate, particularly to Helen in her late stage of pregnancy.

Mary was thirty when she married. Thomas arrived ten months later. The following year she gave birth to a girl, Mary Evelyn, a so called blue baby, who died within a few hours. The baby was born in an Indianapolis hospital and Mary was so distraught that she wasn't sure she wanted to return to Kentland...or to her marriage. When she left the hospital, she went to her parents who were already watching Thomas. Weeks went by. Bernard somehow sensed that a farm of their own, and a beautiful old home could be the carrot that might draw Mary back. It did.

Now fifteen years have passed. As Mary looks out the north facing window and watches the snow blowing down the lane, the sad memories of what brought her to this house mingle with her current satisfaction of country living.

She turns to Helen and says, "I've told you my story. Now tell me what brought you to this house today?"

"We were heading to a party in Gary, hosted by one of Jack's old fraternity brothers. With this storm, I doubt we would have made it anyway. We checked the forecast and thought we'd be able to beat it by a day."

Mary smiles back and says, "I know what you mean about the weather forecast being off. Last night Bernard was sure he'd be able to get home from Midway today. I've noticed something over the years I've lived here. If a weather front comes in from the east, it's usually dramatic. That's what's happening today."

In response, Helen discloses, "To be honest, the party in Gary held little allure for me. I've met Jack's friend and his wife a few times, but they're like so many people I've meet through Jack, not friends as much as contacts. People who you might do business with or they might know people you could do business with. Does the name 'Cooper and Associates' mean anything to you?"

Mary shakes her head no.

"Really, there's no reason why it should but it's the largest Advertising Agency in Indianapolis. Jack started it himself and has put his heart and soul into it. I'm really proud of him. When we first met at I.U. (Indiana University), he didn't know what he wanted to do, but he knew he was going to succeed in whatever that was. I found his confidence very attractive. I still do."

Helen resumes, "Anyway, his friend Peter in Gary is president of Gary Mercantile Bank. Jack's been after that account for years and this invitation made him think he was about to clinch it. So, that's the long answer as to why we were on the road today.

 Switching subjects, Helen says, "Mary, there's something I want to ask. What are your impressions of Sandy and Keith? Something's not quite right there."

"I wondered what you thought."

Helen muses, "She really is a sweet girl. I just want to hug her."

"I know what you mean. She's very pragmatic, the kind of girl who asks for nothing in this world. Maybe that's why we want to hug her; she's probably had very few in her life."

"And when I asked what part of the city they live in, she replied, 'I live in Brightwood,' not we live in Brightwood. I doubt very much if they're married."

Mary asserts, "I certainly hope not. She's so young. What chance do either of them really have if they start a family? I saw this situation so many times when I was working as a social worker. It's not a hopeful story."

Mary then switches to a different subject, and pointing, says, "Down this hallway is a bath and the girl's room. You'll notice that room has two entrances, a door from the living room as well. Anyway, let's state the obvious. You'll be spending the night, and that bedroom will be for you and Jack."

"Thank you."

"I'm going to make some chili but why don't you lie down for a while?"

"Oh, no. I'll help here in the kitchen. There must be something that I can do."

Mary counters, "As Jack said, 'We need to take care of Helen,' and I agree. Besides, this will give me a reason to ask Sandy to come and help."

"I do feel I could use a bit of a rest."

"Before you do, let me change the sheets."

Helen says, "I can manage that."

Mary replies, "No. I'm going to enlist Sandy with helping do that as well."

Helen goes into the living room and says to Jack, "Mary has offered us their downstairs bedroom. We're not going anywhere tonight." She then sits down next to her husband.

Mary has followed Helen into the living room. She asks Sandy, "Would you be willing to help me, dear? Come upstairs with me to get clean sheets out of the cedar closet and we'll change the sheets for Helen and Jack."

Sandy replies eagerly, "I'll change the sheets. I've been changing beds all my life." Sandy follows Mary upstairs.

Jack says, "I'll go out to the car and get our suitcases."

Helen cautions, "I don't want you to aggravate your back any more than you have. There's nothing I really need."

Jack replies in an earnest voice, "You may not need it but I want you to have everything that could make you feel more comfortable."

Joseph pipes up, "Give me the keys and I'll go get your suitcases."

Then Keith chimes in, "Joseph, I'm a little bigger." He turns to Jack and says, "I'd be glad to get them."

Jack isn't quite sure what to say. He finally utters, "I would appreciate that very much, Keith." Then he adds, "Maybe both of you could go. There's a large suitcase and a smaller one."

Joseph is happy to be included.

Jack says, "The keys are in my coat pocket. Joseph, will you show me where you hung it?"

All three get up and go to the back of the house. Jack retrieves the keys and gives them to Keith.

Keith wonders why Mary didn't mention what accommodations she was planning for him and Sandy. But, at the same time, he was glad she didn't because then the subject of their own luggage would come up. They don't have any...other than the paper sack of underwear and socks that Sandy thought to bring with her at the last minute.

A loud knock draws all three to the front of the house.

Chapter 5: A Stern-looking New Arrival

Joseph goes to answer, and Keith and Jack are right behind him. Helen continues to sit in the living room. Joseph opens the door to the man standing there. He's wearing a navy blue cashmere coat and gray dress hat. Even before he opens his mouth, his air of distinction is evident. Joseph says, "Come in."

Jack adds, "Come in and join us." Looking at Joseph he says, "Joseph lives here but the rest of us are orphans of the storm. Mrs. Brow is upstairs but I expect she'll be down any minute."

The new arrival replies, "I'm Chester Higginbotham. I noticed the two cars stranded near the house. They must belong to the two of you. Unfortunately, I had to walk a ways further. My car slid off the road and into the ditch and I honestly didn't know which way to come for shelter. After walking north for fifteen minutes, I could make out the Christmas lights outside this house."

Jack observes cheerfully, "You see, Joseph. There was a very good reason for you to turn on those lights."

Joseph replies, "I'll run upstairs to get Mom." He departs and goes up the enclosed staircase that leads off the dining room.

Jack puts out a hand to shake and says, "I'm Jack Cooper."

Keith, no longer in love with the fake name "Logan," simply says, "My name is Keith." He puts his hand out for a shake and then adds, "I know where Mrs. Brow wants us to hang the wet coats," and takes Mr. Higginbotham's coat.

Chester's wearing gray slacks, a light blue dress shirt, and a blue cardigan sweater. He has salt and pepper hair, more salt than pepper. He is seventy-two, and although he has lived a physically disciplined life, he looks every bit his age. He has an intelligent face but because it has drifted toward stern for so much of his life, his mouth has a slight droop.

A minute later, Joseph and Mary come down the stairs. Sandy is following them with fresh sheets in hand. Mary states enthusiastically, "Welcome to our home this Christmas Eve."

Chester says, "I'm Chester Higginbotham."

Mary responds, "Come into the living room and get comfortable."

As they enter the living room, Jack introduces Chester to Helen.

Sandy is standing behind Mary, arms full. Mary says to Chester, "This is Sandy; she and Keith are our other stranded travelers."

Sandy awkwardly smiles and nods her head in recognition. She then proceeds to the downstairs bedroom to make the beds.

Mary asks Chester, "Would you like coffee or tea?"

Chester replies, "Some steaming hot tea sound's perfect."

Mary notices that Chester is visibly chilled. She tells Joseph, "Go up to the cedar chest and bring down one of those Irish wool blankets. And bring down another pair of your father's wool socks."

Mr. Higginbotham sits on the blue plush chair. Jack joins Helen on the sofa. In a flash, Joseph has returned with a blue plaid blanket and wool socks.

As Chester puts on the warmer socks, Joseph, inquisitive as ever, inquires, "Where did you come from and where are you heading?"

Chester answers, "I'm coming from Indianapolis, and I was heading to Lowell, Indiana, to visit my son."

Joseph asks, "Doesn't it seem strange that you're all from Indianapolis?"

Jack responds, "Joseph, you raise an interesting point. But if you think about it, Indianapolis is, by far, the largest city in the state and we were all coming from that direction. Add to that it's Christmas Eve."

"What does Christmas Eve have to do with it?"

Jack replies, "I'm not sure I'm right, but I think more people would be traveling from a greater distance. On top of that, local people probably have had better sense not to be on the road during this storm."

Mary goes to the kitchen. As she's making the tea, thoughts pass through her mind, "I know this man. He's Judge Higginbotham, Family Court. He must be retired by now." Remembering him from her social work days, Mary further muses, "He wouldn't know me. No reason he should, particularly finding me in this farm house all these years later."

As Joseph and Keith are walking through the kitchen, Joseph says to his mother, "Keith and I are going to the Coopers' car to get their luggage."

Mary comments, "I'm sure they'll appreciate that."

Joseph and Keith get their jackets and Joseph puts on his boots. They leave through the back door.

Back in the living room, Jack asks Chester, "How far did you have to walk?"

"It's difficult to know in the blowing snow...but I know it took me well over an hour to get here."

Jack reflects, "You make me realize how lucky we were. We slid in the ditch to avoid a falling telephone pole. Comparatively, we were quite near this house." Attempting to draw Chester further into conversation, Jack continues, "Quite a storm! All of sudden it seemed like we were in the Arctic!"

Concurring, Chester relates his experience, "A light snow started just north of Lafayette, but as I was passing through a little town, I think it was called Fowler, it really started to pick up. A few miles out of town, I wondered if I should turn back and look for lodgings there. Then I saw a sign that read, 'Kentland, 10 miles.' I was confident I could make that. I wasn't aware how much snow had already fallen as I continued north."

Jack avers, "Mother Nature is humbling. I was sure we could make it to Gary this evening." He glances at Helen and says, "Helen is expecting in a couple of weeks. I should have my head examined."

Chester shares, "My decision to drive up to my son's home in Lowell was an impetuous one. I'm not an impetuous person."

....

Sandy goes to the kitchen and asks Mary, "Are there other beds you'd like me to change?"

Mary replies, "You're too good to be true. Yes, there's the boy's room upstairs as well as the guest room. They're all single beds. Those sheets are on the middle shelf, right side. Again, I really appreciate what a huge help you are."

Sandy says, "I've never been in a home as nice as this. I like being part of it."

Sandy's sentiment is not lost on Mary. She knew many "Sandys" in her social work days and recalled the homes they came from. Her heart goes out to Sandy and wants to get to know her better. With that in mind, she says, "I'm afraid I'm going to continue to take advantage of your good nature. After you're through upstairs, would you mind helping me in the kitchen? I'm going to make chili."

Sandy responds enthusiastically, "I'd love to. I know how to make corn bread. That's what we always have when we have chili at home."

"We'll have to check to see if I have all the ingredients."

Sandy leaves to make the remaining beds upstairs.

Mary takes a cup of tea into the living room for Chester. She then asks, "Would you like a shot of brandy to go with this?"

"No thank you. This should do the trick nicely."

Mary leaves to return to the kitchen and Jack and Chester continue their conversation.

Jack states, "Higginbotham. I knew a Higginbotham in high school. We were on the same track team. I think he was only a freshman or a sophomore but he was such a good hurdler, he was on the senior team. Can't remember his first name."

Chester, very well knowing the answer, inquires, "Could it have been Trey?"

"Yes, that was it. Are you related?"

"He's my son. He's who I was on my way to visit today."

Jack exclaims, "Today is full of coincidences. To think that I would know your son. I didn't really know him well. Shortridge is a pretty big school. What year did he graduate?"

"1931"

Jack replies, "I graduated in 28 so we wouldn't have had classes together. But he sure knew how to clear those hurdles. Both high and low. He was a champion." Switching subjects, "So what does Trey do in Lowell?"

Chester appears to not hear the question and states, "Shortridge is a big school with quite a history."

"I know. I believe it was started during the Civil War."

Confirming, Chester states, "1864. My dad was in one of the first graduating classes, 1871. I graduated in 1901."

Jack interjects, "Sounds like you're an old Northside family."

"We're fourth generation from England. It was my grandfather who moved his family here from Massachusetts. He was an attorney and set up practice on Vermont Street, just off the Circle."

Jack replies, "My family's been in Indianapolis for four generations. My grandfather came from a little town just outside of Pittsburgh. He was originally in the coal business but soon got in the business of installing furnaces. My brother continues to run that business."

"Cooper Heating and Cooling?"

"Yes."

"It must have been your dad who installed the furnace when we first built our home and then your brother when we switched to oil a few years ago. We've been good customers."

After a brief pause, Chester states his concluding thought, "You didn't remain in the family business."

"No. My brother had been groomed to head that business all through our growing up years. I knew that either I'd be working for him or I'd need to strike out on my own. I still didn't know what I wanted to do after college. I got a job selling air time for WIBC (radio). That got me in the door of a lot of businesses as well as the only advertising agency that existed in Indianapolis at the time. Within a year, I knew I wanted to start a second advertising agency and become the dominant agency in the city. It's been a dream come true."

Helen smiles and states, "He's not going to tell you but I will. Jack heads the largest advertising agency in Indiana."

Chester responds, "Sounds very gratifying. It takes courage to follow one's passions. I've known others who have tried but with less fortunate results."

Jack reflects and then says, "I've been lucky. You don't know it as a kid, but I grew up knowing people whom I'd someday do business with. Hook Drugs is my largest account. Hell, the guy who was the silent partner of Bud Hook was the father of a good friend of mine from Shortridge."

Chester ponders to himself, "But you really do know it as a kid. You know some families are more important than others. Just as you know some people are better looking, some people are smarter. People, at least most people, gravitate to whatever's going to make them stronger. Evolutionary forces at play."

But rather than share his thoughts, he says, "People can throw good luck away. Sounds like you haven't."

"The best luck I ever had was meeting Helen while we were at I.U. And believe me; I had to stand in line. There were a lot of guys chasing after Helen."

"I don't remember you standing in line. That was one of the things about you that appealed to me." With a smile, she continues, "Just one of the things, mind you."

Mary is alone in the kitchen when the back door opens and Joseph and Keith enter with the Cooper's luggage. They deliver it down the hall to the girl's bedroom.

At the same time, Sandy walks into the living room and says, "Mrs. Cooper, the beds are ready."

Helen replies, "Thank you, Sandy. I think a little rest will do me good."

As Helen gets up, she feels pain in her lower back. It's been going on all day, but more so the last few hours. The baby has been restless as well. She has been feeling mild contractions for a couple of weeks. The doctor told her that that was normal enough, but that they were false contractions. They seem to be getting stronger now, or is it her imagination?

As she passes through the kitchen, she says to Mary, "I hope you don't mind that Joseph was enlisted to get our luggage. That boy has been in and out of the house all day."

Mary responds, "Are you kidding? He loves it. He likes being in the thick of things and he loves being out in weather like this. He gets that from his dad. Bernard and the boys have a history of bundling up and taking long walks in blizzard conditions. They like to think they're Arctic explorers. The girls have more sense."

Helen passes the bathroom and enters the girl's bedroom. The décor consists of two single beds with matching headboards covered in a gray and white marbleized vinyl. Each headboard has a bookshelf the width of the bed. The chenille bedspreads offer a feminine look. Over against the south windows are two wooden dressers of contemporary design. Helen lies down in the bed nearest the north wall.

Joseph heads into the living room while Keith lingers in the kitchen. Wanting to engage Mary he says, "I'm real grateful, Mrs. Brow. for taking us in."

Mary smiles and says, "Keith, I'm grateful, too. Having you all as our guests is making this a special Christmas for Joseph and me. Joseph thrives on adventure...the slightest little thing. He's happy when the bread man comes up the drive. Think what all of you are doing for him! I've been offering tea or coffee. Any interest?"

"No thank you, Mrs. Brow."

Making an additional offer, Mary says, "I know you have to be chilled from being outside. I can make some hot chocolate. It will only take a few minutes."

'That sounds good, Mrs. Brow." Without exactly understanding, Keith feels his defenses crumbling. It's unfamiliar but it feels good. To keep a conversation going, he says, "That Joseph is sure a good kid. You've done a real good job with him."

"We like him. When you have four children, you realize that they're all very different. Joseph is the most sensitive but maybe the most resourceful. He finds everything interesting...except school of course. And even there, I think he likes it a lot more than he's willing to admit. He gets good grades, but then he knows that's expected of him."

A ripple of anxiety spreads across Keith's chest. He never got good grades. No one seemed to expect him to. When he dropped out of school at age 16, the only reaction was an expectation of his working more hours and bringing in more money.

He had always wanted his mother's love. But her life had been so battered, first by her own parents, followed by the deeply flawed men who came into her life. They took what they could and left. She meant to love her son, but her ability to do so had been reduced to vapors.

Just then Sandy walks into the kitchen. Keith senses that his conversation with Mrs. Brow is suddenly over. As he heads out of the room, Mary says, "We'll bring in the hot chocolate in a few minutes."

Sandy asks, "Now what do you want me to do?"

"Let me gather everything I need for the chili and then we'll look to see if I have everything you'll need for the cornbread. I think I probably have it all. Oh, one thing you can do right now, go down into the basement. When you get to the bottom of the stairs, turn left and go into that room. On the shelves to your immediate left, you'll see jars of stewed tomatoes. Bring up a jar. The tomatoes are from Bernard's garden."

Sandy goes downstairs.

A few minutes pass and Joseph comes into the kitchen. Mary asks, "Would you mind taking this hot chocolate in to Keith? And there's enough in the pot for a cup for you if you want to come back and get it. I don't want you trying to carry them both at the same time." Joseph takes the cup in.

Sandy emerges from the basement with the jar of tomatoes.

She utters, "I was taking a good look at everything you've canned. I counted 112 jars of tomatoes...and it looked like twice as many of green beans. That had to be a lot of work."

"It was a lot of work but when the garden is most bountiful, I often have help from an older woman named Clara. She's done this all her life; I've learned a lot from her. Those tomatoes and green beans that you see lined up on the shelves will last us through the winter. Sometimes when I'm in the basement doing laundry, I look at all those jars all lined up and feel a great sense of satisfaction. Probably if I lived on a farm all my life, I might take it all for granted."

Joseph comes back and silently claims his cup of hot chocolate. He then returns to the living room.

Sandy inquires, "Does your whole family work in the garden?"

"Bernard does most of it. The kids do as little as possible, although Joseph likes digging for potatoes. He says it's like finding buried treasure."

Sandy muses, "I think I'd like to have a garden. I've never lived where that was possible."

Mary asks, "Where you live now; do you have a backyard?"

"A little one."

Mary responds, "I bet there would be enough room to plant a couple tomato plants, maybe some green peppers if you like them."

Sandy suddenly realizes that she's referring to the home she shares with her mother, stepfather, and younger siblings. She doesn't want to continue this conversation because she doesn't want to lie to Mrs. Brow.

Switching subjects, she asks, "Can I check to see if you have everything I need for cornbread?"

"Just tell me what you need and I'll tell you if I have it."

"Corn meal, flour, sugar, oil, and two eggs. Oh, salt and baking powder, but I'm sure you have those."

"Yes, I have it all but let's start on the chili first. Sandy, you're taller than I am. Can you reach up and get the macaroni? With a bunch of hungry kids, I've learned that macaroni helps stretch the chili. Also, bring down a can of kidney beans that's on the same shelf."

Mary starts to boil water for the macaroni. She then goes to the ice box to remove a pound of hamburger. Sandy stands by eagerly for instructions. Mary says, "Would you mind going into the living room and bringing back any empty cups? There's a tray on the counter in the breakfast room."

Mary sits down at the small table in the breakfast room and when Sandy returns, she says, "Put the tray on the kitchen counter and then come back here and sit down. I think we both deserve to rest for a few minutes."

Sandy complies. Mary says, "Tell me about your job at Hooks. How many days do you work in a week?"

Sandy's face is full of consternation. She finally says, "Oh, Mrs. Brow. I don't want to lie to you. I'm still in high school and Keith and I aren't really married."

Mary offers an understanding smile and says, "Sandy, dear, I knew that I liked you as soon as you walked in the door. Just know that. You don't have to explain anything to me."

Relieved, Sandy reveals, "About Hooks. I work around my school schedule. It's usually around 25 hours a week."

Mary responds, "With school on top of it, those are a lot of hours. How do you manage?"

Sandy replies, "I have two study halls and I make the most of that time. My grades are pretty good considering."

"What do you want to do after high school?"

"I'd like to take some business classes. I think I'd be very good as a secretary. My mom wanted to be a secretary but she got pregnant with me. After I was born, they needed money right away so she went to work. Eventually she got hired on at RCA; she still works there."

"RCA on Michigan Street? That wasn't far from where I grew up. Your mom might know my cousin, Katie McCallen; she's been there a long time, too. Your mom must depend on you a great deal. How many brothers and sisters do you have?"

"A sister and two younger brothers. My sister Wanda is 13 and we have the same father. My mom's second husband didn't stick around long and then she married Larry. He's the father of our brothers, half-brothers, and they're just six and four. They're a handful."

Mary surmises, "The water must be boiling by now. Let's get the chili going." The two women get up and go into the kitchen. Mary continues, "Would you open the can of beans? There's an opener in the silverware drawer right in front of you. Also, you might as well take the lid off of the tomatoes. Meanwhile, I'll start frying the hamburger.

"Sandy, I'm just wondering, do you have any time for yourself? Do you ever do anything fun?"

"Not really. When I'm home and Mom's at work, I'm watching the boys. Then Larry expects supper to be ready when he gets home. He's the kind of guy you don't want to disappoint."

"So what about friends?"

"I really don't have any. I guess I'm not a person who's much fun to be around."

"I don't think you're being fair to yourself."

"No, it's true. Even when I was a little girl I didn't have friends. That's why Keith is so different. I know that he really likes me. He told me that he couldn't take his eyes off me from the first time that he saw me. He was working at Hooks as a stock boy. He was working full time because he dropped out of school when he was sixteen. Anyway, I would look up, and there he was, smiling at me. It felt uncomfortable at first but then I started to like it. Keith really has a nice smile if he's willing to let you see it."

Mary responds, "I'm sure you're right. When he was in here just a few minutes ago and I saw a side to him that I liked very much."

Sandy resumes, "He's treated me differently than anyone ever has. He would walk me home, well not exactly home, because we never wanted Larry to see us, but he'd walk me to about a block away. And, he would say the sweetest things, and just holding hands made me feel differently than I had ever felt before."

Mary, directing Sandy, says, "In the lower cabinet to your left, see if you can find the colander and then put it in the sink." She adds, "Once the macaroni is done, we can throw the chili together.

"Then you can make your cornbread. I also have plenty of ingredients for a salad. Thank heaven I was at the grocery yesterday. I was expecting Bernard and the older kids home today, and with Christmas tomorrow, I stocked up."

"I heard from Mrs. Cooper that your husband and older kids were in New York for a funeral...and that they got stuck there because of weather. I'm sorry for the sad reason but I can't help wondering what it must be like for them to be in New York."

"I think they did get to see the huge Christmas tree at Rockefeller Center and the people skating in front of it but not much else."

"But they got to fly on a plane to get there."

Mary doesn't quite know what to say. It's so glaringly apparent that her children have had so many advantages throughout their young lives that Sandy has not. And it's not as if Sandy's sense of awe has provoked envy on her part. She's just sharing her wonderment. But, beyond this most recent exchange, Mary senses that she has opened a channel of communication with Sandy that hasn't been common in her young life. Mary wants to make the most of it and to do so, requires her to move slowly with any counsel. So she simply replies, "Yes, they did have the experience of flying. I haven't had a chance to ask them what they thought of it."

Mary then says, "I think the macaroni's ready," and pours it into the colander.

....

The three men continue to sit in the living room. Jack had gone off on a tangent of how television has turned the advertising business upside down, and for him, it's all been good news. He continues, "When radio was king, clients didn't need our help as much but producing a television spot is much more sophisticated. And since the cost of TV airtime is so much more than radio, it's doesn't make sense to pay that money and then have some hokey spot that makes you and your business look cheap. And, not only that, since you're paying so much more, you want to utilize every second to sell your product or service. For example, we've had a spot for Hooks that's been on since Thanksgiving. It's to get people thinking of various holiday gifts, nice affordable gifts. And since they'll most likely be in a Hooks Drug store anyway, why not take advantage of the trip? We've gotten really good feedback on that spot."

Jack is suddenly aware that he has been commanding the conversation and feels the need to draw Keith in. He asks, "Keith, what do you do?"

"It funny that you've just been talking about Hooks. I used to work there until the end of September but now I have a better job at Kroger. Sandy, she still works at Hooks."

Jack asks, "So, why is working at Kroger better?"

"I'm getting paid more per hour and I'm working more hours. I work inventory."

Jack suspects "working inventory" means stocking shelves and doesn't ask for further detail. He admires Keith as a young man willing to work, no matter at what.

Chester takes the conversation in a different direction. He observes, "Do you know who these people are? The Brow's? They're the hybrid seed corn family. I noticed their billboard just south of the house. Your car, I think, was north of it."

Jack exclaims, "So that's it! Sure! I've seen their field signs all over the Midwest. I've been wondering who they are."

Jack smiles and looks toward Chester, "Now that you answered that question, I have one for you. "What do you do?"

Chester replies, "I doubt it will surprise you if I say that I'm retired, but I had a satisfying career on the bench. I was a Family Court Judge."

This announcement rattles every bone in Keith's body. For the past hour or more, he seemed to forget that he had talked Sandy into running away with him, and that he stole a car to do so. Now he feels trapped as he had never felt trapped before. Trapped in a farmhouse on Christmas Eve with no means of getting away, trapped with a judge sitting five feet away, trapped with the car he stole, now stuck in a ditch.

When he had been out with Joseph to get the Coopers' luggage, the snow that had drifted over Larry's car gave him a false sense, if not of absolution, at least a temporary reprieve. He felt safe for the moment and looked forward to spending the rest of Christmas Eve with Mrs. Brow, Joseph, and the Coopers. He didn't give much thought to the old man who trailed in last. He was just an old man, and like many of his generation, Keith didn't take much notice of older people. Now this guy turns out to be a judge. Retired or not, he poses a threat.

Coming out of his haze of panic, Keith unenthusiastically returns to listening to the conversation of the older man and Mr. Cooper.

Jack asks, "Family Court. What does that mean?"

"It means cases dealing with family law such as divorce, child custody, and domestic abuse. Family court is a civil court so juries aren't involved."

"Can you send someone to jail?"

This question gets Keith's full attention and he's relieved to hear Chester say, "No. That's left to criminal courts."

As relieved as Keith is to hear this, a judge is still a judge. He finally feels he has his breathing under control enough to say, "I think I'll go down to see if, what'd you call it...the stoker...has enough coal."

Jack could have told him that his concerns were premature, that their earlier efforts would suffice for the time being, but he sensed the restlessness in the young man and said, "Good idea, Keith." Keith gets up and leaves the living room.

Jack muses, "That kid has been hard to figure out."

Chester responds, "Something's troubling him."

Jack continues, "When he first arrived, he was all bluster but later, when I was showing him what's needed to keep the furnace going, he was as anxious to please as a puppy wagging its tail. Then you saw how eager he was to get our luggage out of the car."

"Yes, I noticed that about him."

"I think I'll go down to the basement to see how he's getting along." Jack proceeds to the basement stairs, only to find Keith sitting in the same spot that Joseph had occupied earlier. He walks around him, proceeds to the stoker, and declares, "I think we're good for now."

Keith continues to sit there. Finally, he feels the need to say something and his mind goes back to what Joseph had said earlier in the day. He asks, "What did Joseph mean when he said, 'All energy comes from the sun?' You said yourself that the heat comes from the burning coal."

Jack responds, "But where did the coal get its energy? You can trace it back to decomposed living matter, such as a plant or an animal, that got that energy from the sun. I'm talking about millions of years ago.

"And Keith, we're not just talking about energy to heat the house, we talking about all energy, including the energy that fuels you and me. When you eat a hamburger for nourishment, and then you have the energy to get back to work, it's the same story. The cow got the energy by eating the grass, or the corn, or whatever it ate, which had captured that energy from the sun. Plants and trees capture the energy by something called photosynthesis. Don't ask me how that works; I don't remember."

Keith replies, "That's real interesting. They should teach that in school."

"I think they do, Keith. Helen was a school teacher in the early years of our marriage. We'll ask her. She'll do a much better job of explaining it, photosynthesis and all the rest of it, than I have."

Then Keith resumes, "Something else I've been wondering about since I've been sitting here, "How does the stoker know when it should release more coal into the furnace?"

Jack explains, "The stoker is an auger that moves the coal slowly to the furnace. You can control the speed that the auger turns by manipulating the thermostat upstairs."

"How does that work?"

"The thermostat is basically a coiled spring that expands or contracts according to the room temperature. How that works is a little complicated, but it involves two electrical contacts. If I had a thermostat that we could take a part, I could explain it a lot easier."

"I heard Mrs. Brow say that they're going to convert to oil. Why is that better?"

"For one thing, that means the end to hauling scoops of coal to the stoker. So bye-bye coal. Bye-bye stoker. The furnace will be fed by oil from a tank that they'll probably bury outside and it will all be automatic. They'll have to get a new furnace but it will be worth the convenience."

"You sure know a lot about how this equipment works."

"You might have heard me say earlier, I grew up with it."

Jack noticed that Keith's mood had significantly altered for the better since he had left the living room. And that had been Jack's objective in coming down to the basement to be with him. This really wasn't the Jack most people knew. Not that he wasn't capable of caring about others, he just didn't take the time to notice.

Just then they heard Sandy call down the stairs, "Supper's ready."

Jack and Keith go upstairs and after washing their hands, they join Chester, Helen, Mary and Joseph at the table.

Mary says, "Joseph, since you're sitting where your dad usually sits, why don't you say grace?" Joseph complies, and then the simple meal of chili, cornbread, and salad is passed around.

Jack declares, "This chili is really good! I'm not sure how, but I really built up quite an appetite sitting around this afternoon."

Chester agrees, replying, "Yes, everything is quite good."

Mary says, "The cornbread is compliments of Sandy. It's better than my usual attempt. Sandy, I'll appreciate if you write out the recipe."

"I'll try, Mrs. Brow, but when I make it, it's just a little bit of this and a little bit of that."

Helen says, "Everything looks delicious but I don't have much of an appetite."

All of a sudden, there's a knocking on the back door. Somewhat soft in volume, but nevertheless a knock.

Joseph states, "I'll go see who it is."

Mary says, "I'll go with you." They get up from the table and walk to the back of the house.

Chapter 6: The Reluctant Guest

It's dark now but when they get to the back door, there's no mistake that it's a black man's face peering through the door's window.

Joseph is taken back. He had seen black people on his many trips to Indianapolis but had never spoken to one. He certainly never expected to see a black person at his own door.

Mary opens the door and says, "Come in! Come in! My name is Mrs. Brow. This is my son, Joseph. Now, take your wet jacket off and your wet shoes. Joseph..."

Joseph interrupts, "I know, go get a pair of dad's socks."

As Joseph turns to go to the front of the house, the new arrival states, "My name is William, Ma'am."

Mary says, "Well, William, you're very welcome along with our other stranded travelers. As soon as Joseph returns with warm socks, please come in and join us for supper. Hope you like chili and cornbread."

William responds, "I do, Ma'am. Thank you."

Mary replies, "I'll set a place at the table. There's plenty of room."

Joseph is back with the warm socks. William puts them on but then as he approaches the little table in the breakfast room, he says, "I'd think I'd like to sit here."

Mary replies, "If that's what you prefer. But first come into the dining room and meet our other guests. What's your last name, William, so I can introduce you properly?"

"My last name is Paris. William Paris."

William follows Mary into the dining room and introductions are made. The Coopers and Chester greet him warmly. Sandy and Keith are polite but subdued.

Jack pronounces, "You picked the right house. Mrs. Brow and Joseph are wonderful hosts!"

William nods his head affirmatively but then returns to the little table in the breakfast room. Mary soon brings in large servings of the meal.

From where Joseph is sitting, he continues to watch William. He's beaming with excitement of this new experience. He has had so little exposure to negroes. One of the childhood books from the family library was "Turkey Trot and the Black Santa," a story about a poor black family's wondrous Christmas made possible by the adventures of the oldest son.

And, for some reason, Joseph has had an image locked in his mind from a Thanksgiving trip to Indianapolis when he was quite young. It was of a middle-aged negro woman, wearing a threadbare, green, cloth, coat, standing on a corner, waiting to cross. It was obvious that the coat was not keeping the woman warm. Over the years, Joseph had often thought about that woman.

Now here was a negro in his own home. He felt a bit shy but even more exhilarated at the prospect of talking with him.

After dinner, all the guests return to the living room with the exception of Sandy and William. Helen's offer to help with the cleanup is rejected, but Sandy falls right into the task of clearing the table, and then continues with further efforts in the kitchen. After William finishes his dinner, he steps into the kitchen and says, "Mrs. Brow, I'd just as soon go down to the basement."

Mary responds, "I'd wish you'd go into the living room with everyone else. I think you'll like them once you get to know them better."

"It's not that I don't like them, Mrs. Brow. I'm just more comfortable being by myself."

Just then, Joseph comes into the kitchen and says, "Mrs. Cooper has gone to lie down again. And looking at William, he says, "Everyone is wondering where Mr. Paris got stuck." He asks William, "How far did you have to walk?"

Mary says, "William, why don't you go into the living room long enough to satisfy their curiosity? In a storm like this, we all feel we're in this together."

Reluctantly, William follows Joseph while Sandy continues to help Mary in the kitchen.

Once in the front of the house, William grabs a chair from the dining room and places it as much in the dining room as the living room.

Jack states, "William, I hope you don't mind me calling you William, we've all gotten on a first name basis here."

William nods his head in assent.

Jack continues, "So William, we've been wondering, were you traveling north or South?"

"I was traveling south, Mr. Jack. I was heading home to Louisville."

Jack remarks, "Well, that shoots Mrs. Brow's theory that the State Police in Kentland had closed the highway going south. We all were coming from the south, oddly enough, all coming from Indianapolis. Were you the only car you saw stranded?"

"Yes, Mr. Jack. I didn't see any other cars stranded."

Jack continues, "If I may ask, how far did you walk to get here?"

"I'm guessing a quarter mile."

Keith speaks up, "I'm surprised you got that close. We haven't seen any traffic coming from that direction since we've been here."

Joseph asks the question that everyone was starting to wonder? "How long ago did you get stuck?"

"Must been two, three hours ago."

Now the question in everyone's mind is, "Why did William remain in his car for so long?" The adults have the restraint not to ask and Joseph is momentarily distracted.

Chester picks up the conversation, "So your home's in Louisville. Where were you coming from?"

"I was coming from Gary, Mr. Chester. I moved up there almost four months ago and was going back home to Louisville to bring my wife and three kids back with me."

Joseph inquires, "How old are your kids?"

"Six, four, and one."

If anything, the howling wind has become louder. Keith walks around the Christmas tree and looks out of the window. He observes, "The wind is blowing the snow fierce; you can't tell if it's still snowing."

William gets up, takes the chair he had been sitting on back to the dining room table and silently leaves the room. As he passes through the kitchen, Mary also remains silent, this time respecting William's wish to be alone. But less than a minute later, Joseph is following on William's tail. Mary doesn't attempt to stop him.

William settles himself on the step that's usually Joseph's perch. William is a big man, over six feet, thickly built and muscular, but Joseph manages to scoot by him. He sits on a lower step by which he can turn and talk with William. William doesn't seem bothered by his company.

Joseph asks, "Mr. Paris, haven't you seen your children for four months?"

"No, Mr. Joseph."

"Is Gary that far from Louisville?"

"No. And it's not that I didn't want to see them. Be sure of that. But I've been saving up. I needed to get a car that was more dependable before I'd bring my family up. And I needed to save every penny so that we can rent a nice home in Gary."

"Why did you leave Louisville in the first place?"

"Mr. Joseph. There's a lot I wouldn't expect you to understand. Louisville has a southern-city-way-of-thinking which isn't always so good for a negro family. Let's just say that."

Joseph looks at William. It's the first time he's really looked at a black face, that is, really looked. As is his nature, he wants to understand what he isn't expected to understand. His own face reveals both curiosity and empathy. Finally, he says, "Will you be leaving much family behind?"

"No. Our families, me and my wife's, are really from Mississippi. We came to Louisville right after we married. My mother came with us but she passed six months ago. It was after that my wife, her name is Carla, and I decided to make the move further north. I came up to find a good job."

"Did you?"

"Yes. A good paying union job at Gary Steel."

"What do you do there?"

"I'm on a clean-up crew that sweeps up for the whole shift. The pay is real good."

Joseph hears more than William's words. He hears that sweeping floors all day is an improvement over what William's former life had been, and he starts to understand a bit of what he isn't expected to understand.

And he understands more when William volunteers, "I've put down a deposit to rent a house with an indoor bathroom and three bedrooms. That will be a dream-come-true for Carla. It's too bad my mother didn't live to see it."

"I bet you miss your mother."

"Mr. Joseph, I surely do. She raised me along with my two older brothers. Both of them stayed in Mississippi but I'm going to try to get them to come north, too."

"Mr. Paris. Why do you call me 'Mr. Joseph?'"

"That's more of those Southern ways I was talking about. A negro is always expected to show respect to a white person, any white person. That's just an example."

"Please, just call me Joseph," and after hesitating a moment, asks, "and don't you resent the way you're supposed to treat white people?"

William avoids answering and says, "I can see that you're a good boy, Mr. Joseph....Joseph."

"I have another question."

"I bet you do."

"Why did you stay in your car for so long? Weren't you afraid you'd freeze to death?"

"I had the car running and the heat going."

"Then did the car finally run out of gas?"

"You do ask questions! Yes, I finally did run out of gas."

"I'm really glad you came to our house."

"Me, too, Joseph. Now, that I'm here and met you and your mother, me too."

....

Sandy has remained in the kitchen helping to finish the supper dishes. She then sits down at the little table in breakfast room and Mary takes this as an invitation to continue their conversation.

Mary remarks, "You don't ever seem to run out of energy! That's a gift."

Sandy muses, "Part of the reason is that I'm used to having so much to do. Another part is that I'm not real comfortable talking with people, so I guess, I just stay busy."

Mary replies, "I hope you feel comfortable with me."

"I do. Your kids are so lucky to have such an understanding mother."

"I'm not sure they'd agree, but thank you. That's a lovely thing to say. But, there may be another element at play here. Sometimes it's easier to talk to a stranger than someone you know. Not that I want you to think of me as a stranger."

"That's what's funny. I don't think of you as a stranger at all. I feel like I can tell you anything...and not get into any trouble for it. You're not like Mom, and especially Larry; they find ways to make me feel guilty when there isn't any reason for me to feel guilty."

"Sandy, you weren't in the kitchen when Helen and I were having a conversation and I told her that I had been a social worker before I married and moved up here. Part of that job was to be a good listener. So is there something in particular you want to talk about?"

"Oh, yes! Oh, yes! I've got to tell you why I ran away with Keith. We've been having sex. We've gone to his mother's apartment when he knows she won't be there. We've done it three times. And Keith says we've got to get married because no other guy will ever want me now that I've had sex with him."

Mary gently shakes her head no and says, "That's not true. A lot of girls marry someone who was not their first sexual partner. A lot more than you might think. This is nothing against Keith, but sleeping with him is not a reason to run off and marry him."

"But what do I tell Keith? He tells me that I'm the only one in the world who means anything to him. And, to be honest, that's the way I feel, too. I've never really been loved before. I don't want to give that up."

"I understand. If your feelings aren't important, what is? But there are other things to think about, too."

At this moment, Joseph walks in and asks, "Have you figured out where everyone's going to sleep? Look what time it is (the clock on the counter reads 9:08)."

Mary turning to Sandy says, "We'll finish our conversation later." Then addressing Joseph, she says, "I think I've figured that out." Mr. Higginbotham will have the guest room. Keith and William will have the boy's room." Looking at Sandy, she continues, "Sandy can sleep in the second bed in my room, and you get to sleep on the sofa. You're always asking to do that; here's your chance. And since it's Christmas Eve, you can leave the Christmas lights on, both inside and outside, all night."

Joseph couldn't be more pleased and as he returns to the living room. He thinks to himself, "This is going to be a night to remember!"

Chapter 7: Baby Makes a Move

Helen feels her water breaking. She cries out from the bedroom, "Mary, could you come in here?"

Mary is in there immediately and so is Jack who heard Helen's cry from the living room.

Helen says, "I'm pretty sure my water broke."

Jack reacts, "Oh, God! What does that mean? Are you okay? Is the baby okay?"

Mary responds in an even voice, "It means that the baby is going to arrive sooner than you expected...but there's no reason to panic."

Jack, continuing in his exclamatory state, asks, "How can you say that? We're stranded in this house with no way to get a doctor. Oh, my God!"

Mary responds, "Most babies born throughout human history didn't have a doctor to navigate their arrival. It's important that we all be calm. Jack, I've given birth multiple times and I know something about this. Helen's contractions aren't at the frequency that one would even call the doctor."

Helen says, "Jack, I understand that you want to be helpful, but could you go back into the living room? I think I'd be more comfortable with Mary helping me out at this point. If Mary needs additional help, we'll get Sandy."

Jack continues questioning, "But what's happening? The baby wasn't supposed to arrive until another three weeks."

Mary responds, "It's quite possible that the doctor miscalculated the delivery date. The baby may be arriving exactly when it's supposed to."

Jack pleads to Helen, "Don't shut me out. I need to know that you'll be okay."

Mary says, "As soon as you leave, we're going to get Helen into the dry bed and more comfortable clothes."

Helen implores, "Jack, dear. Please go into the other room."

Jack leaves reluctantly.

Mary calls out, "Joseph, run upstairs and get my pink nightgown out of my middle drawer. Then bring me the clock that's on the kitchen counter. Also, the tablet that's by the phone and the pen. But just knock on the door when you have it all."

Mary says to Helen, "We'll time your contractions and we'll have a better idea of what's going on. When it gets down to every five minutes, we'll know the baby is preparing to make its entrance. And, oh, between contractions, try to pant rather than normal breathing. I think you'll find that helps."

Joseph arrives at the door. Because of his recent tutorial on babies being born, he would give anything to peek in, but he knows better.

Mary sets the clock on the headboard. She states, "I can probably witness for myself every time you have a contraction but let me know anyway."

Helen expresses, "I hope Jack can settle down. I know him better than anyone is the world and I know how hard this must be on him."

Mary asserts, "He'll be okay. I know your concern for him is out of love, but for goodness sake, you're the one having the contractions."

"You'll have to be patient with me when it comes to my attitude toward Jack. It's so deeply embedded. He's been my focus for twenty plus years. And it's not so much that Jack demands it as it's something that fulfills a need for me. The first couple of years after we were married, I taught school. I really didn't enjoy it. I didn't know how to handle the kids that were acting out."

Mary comments, "I knew those same kids. But as a social worker, I had a different kind of authority over them that could bring about different consequences...and most of them understood that."

Helen resumes, "And it wasn't just that I didn't like teaching...I realized that I had an easy alterative. This is really going to sound obnoxious, but I've always been attractive...and I've always known it. Even in grade school. Then came high school, Homecoming Queen, that kind of thing, and college with more of the same. I was aware of the old saying, 'It's a man's world,' but I figured I could play it to my advantage.

"Oh, here's another contraction."

Mary says, "I'm timing them. But keep panting."

Helen says, "Again, I don't want to sound obnoxious but for some reason I feel a need to talk about my marriage."

Mary replies, "Sure."

"After my second year of teaching, Jack said to me, 'I don't know why you want to go back to that. If you enjoyed it, that would be one thing...but you don't. You don't have to. I'm making enough money and I'm just going to keep making more. I'd rather you'd help me become the largest advertising agency in Indiana. You always help when you come to dinner with me and a client. They respect me, but take a look at you and they're wowed. We're a great team that way."

"I was so relieved. It allowed me to go back into my comfort zone. I know it must sounds shallow, but life really has been easier for me because of my looks. People don't expect a whole lot more.

"And what I want to say is that Jack has always made me feel special. He's never stopped being in love with me. I know that's not true for a lot of my women friends. The fire goes out and they settle into a different kind of relationship. I'm not saying that's a bad thing, maybe they've moved on to a more mature relationship, but I'm glad that hasn't happened for Jack and me. And Jack is the driving force. Of course this is something we never talk about. He's not 'Mr. Introspection;' he just is. But his 'is' is electric, at least for me."

Mary doesn't know quite what to make of this conversation, particularly when a new mother is feeling contractions. Similar thoughts had definitely not passed through her mind during the five times she had given birth. And if she were to be honest, her romantic relationship with her husband had moved on to the "more mature" stage very early on.

Helen continues, "I really don't know why I'm telling you this about Jack and me. It's really not the kind of thing people talk about...but there's something about you, Mary, that makes it so easy to say anything."

Mary replies, "I'm glad you feel that way. But what's strange is that Sandy said almost exactly the same thing a little while ago. Truthfully, I don't know that I am the kind of person. I was wondering about that when I was with Sandy. I was about to say to her that it was the situation: strangers all of a sudden thrown into an intimate association, like two people inches apart on a long bus ride. But then I realized that she's probably never been on a long bus ride."

Helen, looking at Mary with an anxious look in her face says, "I think my need to talk about Jack has partly been a distraction. Mary, I'm afraid. I'm afraid about the baby."

Mary says in her most reassuring voice, "Oh, don't be. Everything will turn out okay. With Thomas, our first born, he didn't arrive until 36 hours after my water broke. They'll have these roads opened by daybreak and we can get you to Dr. Yegerlehner just minutes after that."

Helen, feeling very vulnerable, discloses, "I want this baby more than anything I've ever wanted. So does Jack. I think we've been afraid to talk about it in case something happens. Yes, Jack wanted to go to Gary so that he could land an important account, but all I would have had to say was, 'I don't think I should make this trip.' He would have understood. I was afraid to. I was afraid I'd make him afraid. This is how crazy it was. I know I indicated earlier that I was indifferent to making this trip, but the truth is I insisted that we go.

"I think we have a reputation in Indianapolis as this beautiful couple on top of the world, one fabulous year following the other. People don't know how hard we tried having a baby the first years of our marriage, seeing one doctor after another. None of them were able to explain why we couldn't, but after five years we accepted the fact that we'd be childless. Maybe that has contributed to our strong attraction to each other, knowing that just the two of us were our family, children wouldn't be part of it. Then last spring while we were on a business trip to Los Angeles, I began to think our luck had changed. I didn't say anything to Jack because I didn't want to get his hopes up. But when we returned to Indianapolis, I went to the doctor and the pregnancy was confirmed.

"I made a special dinner that night, and Jack asked me, "What's this all about?" I said, "Well, I'm going to have a baby in January and I don't know if I'll have the time to do this kind of thing anymore." Then I started to cry and Jack started to cry. I'd never seen him cry before. He came over to where I was sitting and I stood up and we just clung to each other sobbing. That was the happiest moment of my life."

Mary says softly, "That's beautiful."

Meanwhile, Jack and Chester are having a very personal conversation of their own in the living room.

Jack laments, "I can't believe that I was such an ass to think this trip to Gary was a good idea. I thought I had a good chance of cracking the Gary Mercantile Bank account by attending tonight's party of an old fraternity buddy's. I've waited years for this opportunity but that doesn't mean I couldn't have waited longer."

Chester responds, "You're a businessman. I'm sure that part of your success is making a move when a door is open. Did I hear Helen say earlier that you're the number one advertising agency in Indiana? That's no accident. You made that happen."

Jack responds, "Yes, I'm ambitious, always have been. As I said earlier, there was never a question about me and my brother working together. I never would have been happy with the number two position and I wouldn't have allowed anyone else peace of mind. At least that's one mistake I didn't make. But this whole thing today was irrational on my part."

Chester counters, "Don't you think Helen would have said something if she thought running up to Gary wasn't a good idea?"

Jack replies, "Helen's attitude is usually, 'to get along, just go along,' but there was something strange about this morning. She practically insisted that we go."

"Well, she was certainly in a superior position to judge if the baby was soon on its way."

"Chester, what else are you going to say to me? Of course you'll try to make me feel better. But this account could have waited. Hell, if I never got it I'd still have the largest advertising agency in Indiana by a long shot. Maybe I should be allowed to question my judgement at least for a moment. It might do me good."

Chester continues his attempt to offer comfort, "I'm certainly not an expert about these things, and I've only had one child, but there was at least fifteen hours between the time my wife's water broke and Trey arriving on the scene. I remember because I was there. Eleanor was actually already in the hospital when her water broke. Hospital stays were a lot longer in those days." Chester didn't want to go into the story that Eleanor's rheumatic fever as a child had left her with a weak heart and having a baby was putting her life in peril. "I stayed with her until she went into delivery and then I was shoved out with all the other expectant fathers.

"What I'm trying to tell you is that there's a good chance these roads will be cleared within a few hours. I stepped outside while you were talking with Helen and Mrs. Brow, and I'm pretty sure it's stopped snowing. And even if they don't have the telephone pole off the road right away, you could drive into Kentland. The boys and Mr. Paris could dig out the driveway. I'm sure Mrs. Brow would let you use her car."

Jack replies, "Thanks, Chester. You know, ever since I was a kid, I've had two approaches to a problem. One is to work on it until I figure it out. The second is to distract myself until a solution starts to become apparent. For now, I'll have to go the second route...so help me distract myself."

Jack assumes Chester's wife is deceased...he wouldn't be on the road Christmas Eve without her. So, he simply says, "Tell me about your family."

"It was just Eleanor and our son Trey. Eleanor has been gone eleven years now."

"That's has to be hard, even eleven years later."

"To be honest. Especially during the holidays. But I was lucky to have her as long as I did." This conversation wasn't easy for Chester; he had always been a very private person. But he realized he had a role to play in helping Jack manage his anxiety. He continued. "Eleanor and I had known each other since we were kids at Central Avenue Methodist Episcopal Church. She had a weak heart even then, but she always had a very loving heart. Sometimes I wondered if her own fragility made her so sensitive to others...but really, I think she would have always been the way she was."

He wants to add, "When I was first on the bench, I thought environmental factors played the major role in how a person develops, but as the years went on, I became more of the mind that, primarily, we are who we are from the womb." However, he doesn't want to refocus Jack's mind on his child's impending birth, so he keeps this thought to himself.

He continues, "Eleanor was the only woman in my life, even from childhood. We were the same age and we knew we wanted to spend our lives together by the time we graduated Shortridge. Her family wasn't as affluent as mine and few women of our generation pursued a college education. She wanted to be my wife and I wanted to be her husband and we didn't think beyond that.

"She got a job at the downtown library. And even from the beginning, they understood she was fragile and didn't have her running around and carrying books. But they gained something special in return, someone sitting behind the checkout desk with a smile for everyone. A sincere smile. She worked there while I went through Butler, then law school at I.U. right up until we married."

Jack reflects, "I think you and I both lucked out with the women we married."

Chester nods his head in agreement.

After a brief quiet, Jack says, "I could picture your son Trey while we were talking about him but that's about it. What was it like raising a son?"

Chester utters, "He was a good kid."

Jack senses that Chester is being evasive but that's his business. He was about to take the conversation into a different direction when Chester reclaims it. "I'm going to be honest. Trey was a disappointment and although he never said it, I'm sure I was a disappointment to him. My dad was a lawyer, I was a judge, and I fully expected Trey to follow in our footsteps.

"It was my goal to give him every advantage to do so. On that score, he was a disappointment all the way through. He was a mediocre student in grade school, then he struggled at Shortridge. That's probably why you only knew him on the track team, the only thing he did well there. He was accepted at IU but basically flunked out. He was in the army during the Second World War, and served under Eisenhower at the Battle of the Bulge. Eleanor was so proud of him but she worried so. She didn't live long enough to see him come home.

"One of his army buddies was from Lowell. His dad has a construction company. A big one. Among other things, they build roads and bridges. Trey's buddy had no interest in the family business. Ironically, he came home and studied law and is practicing in his home town. It's Trey who went to work for the dad. Eventually, he married the boss's daughter and they have two daughters. Another irony is that it looks like Trey will take over that business."

Jack asks, "Are you closer with him now?"

"No. My disapproval of him has been so engrained. It was the one strain in my relationship with Eleanor. She always saw how unfair I was to Trey and it hurt her deeply.

"I even blamed him for her death. It was irrational but I thought that if he hadn't gone off to war, she wouldn't have worried so much and maybe she could have lived a little longer. I blamed him for his enthusiasm to serve his country. I ignored the fact that he was of age when he would have been drafted had he not enlisted. I blamed him for getting injured during the first week of that battle at Elsonborn Ridge. We received a telegram notifying us that Trey had been injured, and Eleanor died the following day. When I said that Eleanor has been gone eleven years, it was eleven years this week, December 1944.

"So, instead of being proud of Trey's service to our country, that he was awarded a Purple Heart, I've managed to begrudge him for it. You can imagine what kind of relationship I've developed, or haven't developed, with his wife and children. Finally, they stopped inviting me for holiday visits and that was fine with me.

"Then yesterday, I happened across the movie "The Christmas Carol" on TV. Early in the story, Scrooge's nephew drops by his office on Christmas Eve to invite him to Christmas dinner the following day. Scrooge declines, stating that he had never approved of his nephew's marriage.

"Finally after all these years, I really saw myself. I was Scrooge. Here I am a lonely old man, alienated from his son and his son's family. And why? Because Trey dared to be someone different from whom I wanted him to be. Professionally, I've often counseled parents to encourage their children to develop what skills they enjoyed, what comes naturally to them. But I was too pigheaded to see it in my own family. I had a son who loved taking his bike apart and putting it back together again, who built a birdhouse of his own design at the age of nine, who learned on his own how to mix cement so that he could patch holes in our driveway.

"He loved his mother so much and I think he understood how much she wanted me to love him; he felt the burden that he wasn't able to make that a reality. I remember the morning we drove him to the train as he was about to ship off to Europe. Eleanor was in the front seat and Trey in the back. She had such a warm smile on her face but it didn't hide her tears. I saw in the rear view mirror that he had tears, too. As for me, I just drove emotionless. "And as I told you, she never saw him again."

A moment passes and Jack says, "I'm glad that you're making an effort to reconcile with Trey because it sounds like the right thing to do for both of you. Also, from what you've told me about him, I like him.

"And I have my own personal reason to wish him well. He fought in the war and was decorated. I was ineligible because of my old football injuries. You read me as I am. Ambitious. But I've also had qualms that I had the opportunity to get my advertising career rolling while others were waylaid and could only compete with me after they came home. I'm glad Trey has found the career path that sounds right for him."

....

Mary says to Helen, "I'm going to excuse myself for a moment and make a fresh pot of coffee. I don't know who else might need some but I know I do. I'll ask Sandy to come in and record the contractions."

Mary goes to the kitchen and starts preparing the coffee. Joseph and Keith are sitting at the table in the breakfast room. Mary is surprised but pleased to see that William has joined them. She asks, "Isn't anyone going to bed tonight?" Joseph replies, "Too much excitement. And remember how late I slept this morning." Neither of the men reply.

Mary is more concerned about the baby's imminent arrival than she lets on. Would the roads be cleared in the next 24 hours, never mind by day break? And if the baby comes sooner, could she handle it successfully? What if some complication arose? And an emotion that had been in the back of her mind comes forefront, the deep sadness she had felt at losing her oldest daughter, Mary Evelyn, only a few hours old.

Joseph wanders into the kitchen. Mary says to him, "Remember when we were talking about how babies are born?"

Joseph, quick to engage in such a dramatic subject, responds "Yes."

Mary continues, "I don't think I told you that in olden years, doctors didn't usually deliver the babies. Midwives did. They were women in the neighborhood that had special training. Claire Hassett was one of those women. I think she helped deliver some of your aunts and uncles."

Joseph asks, "Is she the old lady that lives on Carton road?"

"Yes. It's too bad there isn't a way to get her over here."

Joseph thinks about it for a few seconds, and then with excitement, exclaims, "But there is!"

Chapter 8: An Adventure

Joseph continues, "Mr. Hassett brought horses and a sleigh to school last week to show them off. When I told Dad about it, he said that the sleigh was reworked from the old school hack he and some neighbor kids used to get back and forth to school."

Mary responds, "But Joseph, even if they could get over here, there's no way to contact them as long as the phone's dead."

Joseph declares, "Oh yes there is. I could walk over there and ask them to come. It's only a little over a mile. You know how I love being out in this kind of weather."

Mary opposes vigorously, "No, Joseph. Not in the pitch of night. You're being very brave but I couldn't let you do it."

Joseph steps outside the back door and quickly returns. He asserts, "It's stopped snowing. I can do it."

Mary counters, "But Joseph, who knows how badly the country roads have drifted...and will continue to drift?"

The conversation is being overheard in the breakfast room. Keith pipes up, "I could go with him, Mrs. Brow."

William's deep voice joins in, "Mr. Keith, no doubt you're a strong man. But I'm a lot bigger man. I'm taller and my legs are long and strong. Mrs. Brow, if you allow Joseph to go, I'll take care of Joseph. I promise you that."

Mary is deeply moved by the offer of these two men, disparate in their own life stories but now sharing a heroic bond. She replies, "I'm so moved by both of you for your offer, but I can't allow Joseph out into this wild night."

Joseph pleads, "Mom, please let me go. This will be the greatest adventure in my life."

William repeats, "I promise you that Joseph will be safe."

Joseph begs, "Please, Mom. This would be the greatest Christmas present ever."

Mary softens and says, "Let's go into the living room and have a conversation with Mr. Cooper and Mr. Higginbotham."

The three of them proceed into the living room and Mary outline's the possible line of action. Jack's first impulse is to say that he should accompany Joseph. Mary, rather than pointing out Jack's physical limitations, says, "I think Helen would prefer that you stay nearby." She reiterates, "Both Keith and William have volunteered to accompany Joseph, and William, because of his size and strength, makes the more persuasive candidate."

Keith interjects, "Trust me. I'll keep the furnace running, Mr. Cooper. You've taught me a lot today."

Jack responds, "I don't know what to say. We were all total strangers a few hours ago, now this…"

Joseph cuts in, "William, Let's get going before Mom changes her mind."

Mary says, "Joseph, get one of dad's stocking caps for William. And make sure you wear your gloves that have the rabbit fur lining."

Joseph replies, "Okay." Two minutes later, they are out the door.

Mary is anxious about her decision to allow Joseph to go, but at the same time, is confident in William's ability to take care of him. She returns to Helen and explains the turn of events.

Instead of feeling reassured, Helen has a wave of anxiety. She questions, "Mary, are you afraid for me and the baby?"

Mary replies, "No. I just thought we might have an additional layer of safety. My guess is that they'll be back with Mrs. Hassett within an hour and a half."

Helen isn't reassured when she reflects that Mary is allowing her 10 -year-old son to face such brutal elements. Reading her thoughts, Mary says, "Joseph begged me, saying that it would be the greatest adventure of his life. And you haven't had the exposure to William that I have.

He promised that he'd take care of Joseph and I have full confidence that he will."

Sandy has remained in the room. Mary turns to her and says, "Sandy, dear, it's going to be a long night. Can you go in the living room and ask the men if they might like some of the Christmas cookies along with coffee or tea, or anything else they might want? There's some lunchmeat in the ice box and you'll find bread in the breadbox on the counter in the breakfast room. There's some left over corn bread, too." Sandy departs.

Helen discloses, "I heard an earful from Sandy. She told me about her relationship with Keith. It doesn't sound as if she thinks she's pregnant."

Mary comments, "She's confused. She thinks she loves Keith but I think she also wants to go back home."

Helen's mind returns to her husband and asks, "How is Jack holding up?"

Mary replies, "He's anxious as you might expect but Judge Higginbotham appears to be a good counterbalance. I don't know what they've been talking about."

Helen inquires, "Judge?"

"Yes. A family court judge. I haven't mentioned to you that I knew the judge back in my social work days. He had a reputation for being firm but fair. I want him to have a conversation with Keith and Sandy. I think they'd listen to him."

At that moment, Helen had another contraction. Now they were about eight minutes apart.

Helen cries out as quietly as possible and then states, "I don't want Jack to hear me. He'd be so apprehensive." Then she quietly laughs to herself, "Remember when we were talking about it's a man's world. I'm sure of it at a moment like this!"

Mary smiles in agreement.

Helen inquires, "How have you learned to deal with being a woman in a man's world?"

Mary responds, "I'm not convinced I like the idea of it being a man's world."

Helen is surprised by Mary's frank attitude. She wasn't going to pursue the topic but Mary continues. "I hope I'm not shocking you but I think there are some marriages that are built on the husband and wife relationship, other marriages that are more focused on raising a family. Mine is the latter." Mary smiles at Helen and says, "Of course it doesn't have to be either/or. I don't think that will be the case for you."

Helen doesn't comment and an interlude of silence ensues.

Mary finds herself thinking about her parent's marriage. There was no question that her mom was in charge. Her dad drank into despair at times, and as a child, Mary once overheard him threaten to kill himself. The moment was so ingrained in her mind that she remembered exactly where she was sitting on an upstairs step. Mary admired her mother's strength but it was her dad she loved the most. He was kind and intellectually curious, two qualities that her mother, who had known starvation in Ireland, did not hold high on her priority list.

Her thoughts drift to her own marriage and what had been her initial impressions of Bernard. He was a lot like her father: kind and intellectually curious. His quest for learning was probably what drew her to him the most. But over the years she had thought him as "very German", which in her mind could be pejorative. Yes, he's been an excellent provider but regarding their financial situation, he doesn't share with her any more than he wants her to know. She hasn't liked that. She hasn't liked that at all.

"He had also come into their marriage with expectations she found oft-putting. The week they returned from their honeymoon, he brought her a pair of shoes to shine. Maybe one of his younger sisters might have been compliant with such a task, but she handed them right back. And so it has been; quiet maneuvering between the two that has defined their marriage, without ever having a real conversation on the matter. Mary wonders if this is how it is with most couples. She surmised that it is.

Helen moans. Mary becomes quietly alarmed. This latest contraction is at a six minute interval. The baby's journey appeared to skip the milestone of a contraction of every seven minutes. Mary tries visualizing where Joseph and William might be at this moment and doubts if they had reached the Hassett house. Then they will have to hitch the horses and embark on what might be a twenty minute journey.

An unrelated thought runs through her mind. She states, "Helen, will you excuse me? I'll ask Sandy to come in and time your contractions. I'll be right back."

Mary leaves and Sandy takes over. Mary goes into the living room in which Jack and Chester are the only occupants.

Jack anxiously asks, "How is Helen?"

Mary responds, "She's remarkably calm for an about-to-be-first-time-mother. You should be proud of her." Mary then inquires, "Where's Keith?"

Jack replies, "He's in the basement. He's assumed responsibility for keeping the furnace running quite seriously. He's really a very earnest young man when you get to know him."

Mary asks, "Do either of you want a drink from the liquor cabinet? It might help you get through the next few hours."

Chester responds, "I'm not much of a drinker but I seem to be someone quite different from my ordinary self tonight. I'll have one."

Mary says, "The liquor cabinet is in the front entrance way. Help yourself to anything that interests you."

Jack replies, "I'll pass."

Chester goes into the front entrance hall but remains within earshot while he makes his drink.

Mary states, "Keith and Sandy are the real reason I came out here. They're a runaway couple and I'm concerned the road they've been on today is one that could destroy their young lives. And Chester, I know you were Judge Higginbotham from Family Court. I was a social worker in Indianapolis before I married and moved up here. You adjudicated some of my clients."

Chester is now back in the living room. He doesn't pretend to remember Mary but simply says, "What a small world!"

Agreeing, Mary adds, "Yes, when you think that we'd all end up here tonight. Anyway, they're not married. Keith is a high school dropout and Sandy's at risk of doing the same. Judge Higginbotham, I want you to have a chat with them."

Chester inquires, "What more do you know about them?"

Mary replies, "They've been sexually intimate and that's how Keith talked Sandy into running away...that no other man would ever want her after that. Also, Sandy works part time at Hooks but then is practically an indentured servant at home. She never knew childhood; you know that story. I don't really know much about Keith but I can guess he's come out of a fractured home as well."

Chester states, "If such a moment presents itself, I'll do what I can."

Mary's about to return to Helen when they hear a knock on the back door. Is it possible that Joseph and William are already returning with Mrs. Hassett? And if so, why would they be knocking? The three go to the backdoor. Mary opens it to find William carrying Joseph. She cries out, "What's happened?"

Joseph replies in a weak voice. "I'm okay, Mom. My legs just gave out."

William sets Joseph down in a chair in the breakfast room and says, "The drifts were just too much for him, Mrs. Brow."

Mary utters gratefully, "William, you promised that you'd make sure Joseph would be safe and you have."

What no one is saying but everyone is realizing: Mrs. Hassett will not be coming.

William reads their minds and says, "My mother was a midwife and she delivered all three of my children. Actually I delivered the last one. Mama was in the room but I knew what to do because I was with her when the two oldest were born. I could do it again if need be." Looking at Jack, he says, "If you'd trust me."

Jack cries out, "Yes, of course I'd trust you."

Mary says to her son, "Joseph, I'm going to make some fresh cocoa to warm you. Then I want you to go upstairs and lie down in my bed. You don't have to go to sleep but I want you to lie down for a while."

Joseph says resignedly, "Alright, but you have to promise that if I fall asleep, you'll wake me up if the baby is born. That would be the most exciting thing that ever happened!"

Mary smiles and says, "I promise." And then turning to William, she asks, "Can I get you some cocoa as well?"

William replies, "That sounds good, Mrs. Brow."

Mary adds, "William, after you drink your cocoa, feel free to lie down in one of the beds in the boy's room. That should help warm you."

William's mind is elsewhere. "Mrs. Brow, if the baby does come tonight, there are some things we need to have ready. We'll need towels and blankets to keep the baby warm once it arrives. You'll need to wash the mama down to prevent infection so you'll need to boil some water to sterilize those clothes. You'll need another pot of boiling water to sterilize the scissors we'll use to cut the cord."

Mary asks Sandy to stay with Helen while she gathers together everything William said would be needed. She then returns to Helen, and Sandy returns to the living room. By this time, Keith has come up from the basement. Once again, he's starting to feel relaxed. It doesn't last long.

Chapter 9: The Judge Speaks

Chester states, "I'll just come out and say it, Mrs. Brow asked me to have a talk with you two."

Keith's face blanches. He asks, "What about?"

Chester continues, "Mrs. Brow has taken quite a liking to both of you. We all have. Seems that you've been eager to help out in every way possible since you arrived. Now Keith knows I'm a retired Family Court Judge" but looking at Sandy, "I don't know if you do."

Sandy, feeling some apprehension, says, "No."

Chester resumes, "Now family court isn't a criminal court. It deals with family matters. Problems people have in their families. Mrs. Brow actually remembers me from her days as a social worker. Anyway, Mrs. Brow doesn't think that you're really married. Is she right?"

Keith remains silent but Sandy, very appreciative that the truth is in the open without Keith knowing she had already disclosed it, says, "Yes, she's right. Mrs. Brow's really smart, isn't she."

Chester states, "It may seem like none of my business, but the truth is I'm glad you're not married."

Looking at Sandy, "I'm going to ask one more very personal question, Are you pregnant?"

Keith remains speechless as Sandy replies, "No I'm not. I'm sure I'm not."

Chester says, "Again, I'm glad that you're not." And looking at Keith, he says, "It's not any judgement against you. As I've said, I like you. Really, I do."

Keith's face indicates anxiety but also a willingness to listen.

Jack has remained in the room and Keith is glad to have him there. He thinks of Jack as an ally. Jack realizes that this is the conversation that Mary asked Chester to have, and remains silent.

Chester continues, "But since Mrs. Brow asked me to speak with you, I've had a little time to think of how many times I wished that I had a chance to address a young couple before they made choices. Choices that closed off so many opportunities for the rest of their lives. Maybe being stranded together in this farm house was meant to be. Finally, I'm being given that opportunity.

"Now, I want each of you to tell me about yourselves. Sensing that Keith would be more reluctant, he says, "Sandy, let's start with you."

Sandy asks, "What kind of things do you want to know?"

"Your family. Your education. What you'd like to do with your life. Those kind of things."

"I live with my mom, stepfather, one sister and two step brothers. I'm a sophomore in high school and I want to work in an office someday. Oh, I'm working now at Hooks between 20 and 25 hours a week."

"How about your biological dad? Do you have a relationship with him?

"I barely remember him. He took off and that was it."

"How do you get along with your stepfather?"

"It's okay if I do everything he expects me to do. I don't think that he really likes me. He doesn't act like it."

Chester eyes turn to Keith and states, "Okay. Keith, your turn."

"Judge, I really don't like talking about this kind of stuff."

"In the first place, I'm no longer a judge; I'm Mr. Higginbotham. Or better yet, call me Chester. Keith, I'm just this old guy seeing a chance to talk to a young couple. Maybe it's the drink I've just had that's relaxing me, but I really want to have a personal conversation. When I was on the bench, I never had this kind of opportunity. Please give me that chance."

Keith hesitantly replies, "Okay. Same kind of questions you asked Sandy?"

"Yes, please."

"Like Sandy, I barely remember my father. He left and then we lived with my grandmother for a while. After that Mom has had lots of boyfriends that we've lived with. Mom drinks too much. That's part of the reason I dropped out of high school at age 16; I'm 19 now...I needed to bring in more money."

"What kind of job would you like to have if you had the right training?"

"Something kind of technical. I'm good with my hands."

Jack breaks his silence and asks, "How would you like to work for my brother in the heating and cooling business? I could recommend you."

"Thanks, Mr. Cooper. But who wants to hire a high school dropout? I'm a loser and I know it."

Chester counters, "Don't let yourself think that way. Have you ever heard of a GED, a General Education Diploma?"

"I didn't do that well when I was in school. How would I ever pass a test like that?"

Jack interjects, "If you really wanted to, you could. No one opened a door and said, 'Jack Cooper, here's the largest advertising agency in Indiana; it's all yours.' And Keith, it is all mine, but only because I really wanted it. If you really want to pass that test, I know a way you could do it."

"How?"

"Remember, I mentioned that Helen used to be a school teacher? She could tutor you if you really made a commitment."

Keith's face brightens only to quickly fall into despair. Both Chester and Jack took notice but didn't question Keith. Instead, Chester continues with his discussion. "Think about it. If you married now, Sandy probably wouldn't finish high school and you'd probably have a baby before you could afford being parents.

"Keith, you wouldn't have the time to get your GED. You'd be stuck in low wage jobs that would keep you living in poor neighborhoods where your child or children would grow up without seeing a way out. In the same way you, Keith, have grown up without seeing a way out. You've never really expected anything more. Am I right?"

Keith doesn't know how to answer. The concept that he had options rather than just reacting to life's challenges has never been in marrow.

The look on Keith's face is answer enough for Chester and he continues, "Sandy, what's the possibility that you'd ever work in an office if you run off and get married? Be honest with yourself."

Sandy responds, "That's what happened to my mom. It had been her dream to work in an office but after she had me, she didn't finish high school."

Chester suggests, "And maybe that affected the kind of men who came into her life. What do you think?"

But before Sandy can answer, Keith, feeling very defensive, says, "Are you saying, 'Sandy, you can do better than Keith; move on while you can.' I know I'm not good enough but Sandy's the only person who means anything to me."

"No, Keith, I'm not. I'm saying you're two good people who deserve to have good lives. I'm saying both of you have an opportunity to change the direction of your lives so that you can have so much more. But I'm also saying that you have to break out of the cycle of one generation after another, settling for too little."

"No disrespect, Judge, but that's easy for you to say. Were you ever beaten up by your mom's boyfriends, and she was so drunk, all she could do was watch? Did you sneak some of the money you earned from delivering papers so that you could buy cans of tomato soup and hide them under your bed?

"And Mr. Cooper...Jack, no offense...but you probably wouldn't have that advertising agency, no matter how much you wanted it, if you didn't go to college and come from a rich family. You wouldn't even know how to talk like you do."

Jack, uncharacteristically reserved, just offers Keith a look that says, "You have a point."

Chester remains undaunted and not wanting to lose his momentum, continues, "But, you're making my point, son. I'm saying that you don't have to live that way. I'm saying the way to have more is to look ahead, decide what you really want and then have the discipline to do what you need to get there.

"Sandy, that would mean finishing high school and then taking some evening classes to develop some office skills. And, in the meantime, no babies.

"Keith, that would mean getting your GED. We'll see if Mrs. Cooper will help you."

Jack responds, "I know she will. And I'm pretty sure I can find you a job with my brother after that."

Chester adds, "And one thing for sure. If your mother keeps drinking, that doesn't mean you owe her the rest of your life."

Looking back and forth from Sandy to Keith, he summarizes. "I'm saying hold off getting married until you're better set for better lives...and also have better odds for a successful marriage."

Sandy appears both relieved and hopeful. Keith, however, has the discouraged look of one whose life is unraveling.

....

As if timed for a fresh interlude, they hear Mary call out to William who is sitting in the breakfast room, "William, will you come here?"

William comes immediately and so does Jack.

Mary asserts, "I think the baby's on its way."

William asks, "What's the timing of the contractions?"

Mary responds, "They're at three minutes but the speed that they went from four to three suggest that the baby's in a hurry."

Jack cries out, "Oh my God! Dear God, please protect my wife and my baby!"

Helen, trying arduously not to betray her pain and her own anxiety, says. "It will be fine, Jack."

Jack implores, "Please, can I stay?"

Helen says, "Oh, Jack, honey, I want you to."

Jack looking at William, "I won't be in the way, I promise."

"Sure, Mr. Jack. You won't be in the way. You can hold Mrs. Cooper's hand and give her some of your strength."

"No more Mr. Jack or Mrs. Cooper. We're Jack and Helen." Jack is now holding Helen's hand, and he continues, "William, I can't say I've been a very religious man but your showing up at this house tonight has made me a believer."

Helen in her weakened voice adds, "On Christmas Eve."

....

Meanwhile, back in the living room, Chester suggests to Keith and Sandy, "It seems like an invasion of privacy to be listening to a baby being born. Why don't we go upstairs? If they need us for any reason, I'm sure they can find us."

They climb the stairs. All three are beyond exhaustion but are charged with so much adrenalin, sleep is not a consideration. Careful not to wake Joseph as they pass his parent's bedroom, they go into the guest room, at the end of the hall. It's furnished with a single bed, a chest of drawers, and a desk with matching desk chair. Chester sits on the bed, Sandy on the desk chair, and Keith on the desk, his short legs dangling in a nervous fashion.

Chester states, "I can't help but notice your anxiety, son. Do you think it would do any good if you told me about it?"

Keith's mind lurches. He thinks, "Here we go again." But he says, "I appreciate your wanting to help but I think I'm talked out for today."

Chester reflects on how little Keith has had to say, at least about himself, but respects his wishes.

Sandy breaks the silence and exclaims, "Keith, why don't you tell him?"

Keith shoots back, "Sandy, can't you keep your mouth shut!"

There's an uneasy quiet. Chester just sits there trying not to look at either. This deafening stillness belongs to the two of them.

Just then they hear the door to the stairway open and Jack shouting, "Are you up there, Sandy? William says you're needed."

Sandy again is relieved to be rescued from a tense situation. Not wanting to wake Joseph, she replies in a voice just loud enough to be heard, "I'll be right down." She hastily leaves the room.

Chester and Keith are now alone. Chester isn't saying anything and this silence is making Keith feel like the top of head is going to blow off. Finally, he says, "I'm just a damn loser. Always have been. Always will be. There's a reason why I'd never be able to go to work for Mr. Cooper's brother. Please don't ask me why."

After a moment's thought, Chester counters, "Just let me say this. If you're in some kind of legal trouble back in Indianapolis, it might be more than luck that we've been thrown together tonight. Even though I'm retired, I have quite a bit of influence in the judicial system."

Finally, Keith blurts out, "What can you do about me stealing Sandy's stepfather's car so that we could run away? It was a spur of the moment decision that's going to ruin the rest of my life."

Chester responds, "Keith, you're right to realize that this is a serious matter. I'm not going to pretend it's not. But just off the top of my head, I can think of two things I can do for you...but you honestly have to answer this question: Do you have a prior criminal record?"

"No sir."

"Good. Here's what I have in mind. First, when I can get to a working phone, I'll call Sandy's stepfather and explain that you took his car but now you want to return it. Maybe the fact that I'm a judge might persuade him to withdraw any charges that he has already filed. It wouldn't be the first time that I've been able to help someone in this way.

"Second. If that doesn't work and the charges remain against you, I'll be a character witness on your behalf. That might reduce your sentence to probation. I've never done that before but I'm willing to do it for you."

Keith's brown eyes well with tears. He asks, "Why are you willing to do this for me?"

Chester replies, "Because I think you deserve a break in your life. But here's a condition, I want you to stop thinking of yourself as a loser. Start thinking of yourself as someone who deserves a better life like we talked about before."

Keith has an uncertain look on his face.

Chester continues, "What if I told you that everyone feels like they're a loser at times in their lives? They need to think differently to move beyond it. What if I told you that I've been just as big a loser and am just now coming out of it?"

Keith asks doubtfully, "How could you be a loser?"

Chester responds, "I was a rotten father to my son Trey. Not just some of the time, almost all the time. Worse yet, I blamed it all on him even as he tried being the best son he could. What really made me a loser was that I was a family court judge, a supposed expert on family matters. I had this discussion with Jack earlier this evening and got a lot off my chest.

"But there's one thing I didn't tell him. I didn't admit what a coward I was earlier today. You see, just a few miles south of here, I lost my courage to follow through on my surprise visit to Trey and his family. I think I even blamed that on Trey, feeling that he had left me a lonely old man. So I had a new plan to get as far as Kentland, find a motel room, and then turn around and go back to Indianapolis in the morning.

"But now I can see I was just lacking courage. When I get my car out of the ditch, I'm going to head to Trey's and face whatever kind of reception awaits me. I'm a little fearful what that might be...but I also feel so much better because I've changed my thinking on the matter. That's what I want you to do. And I so badly want to hear from you in future years to learn about the success you'll be making in your life."

Keith reacts, "Gee Judge...I'm sorry but I feel I have to call you Judge...I can't remember anyone really expecting me to succeed. Oh, a few teachers, but they soon realized I wasn't much of a student and that dried up."

Chester expounds, "The important thing is that you expect it of yourself. Maybe if we stay in touch, I can help you do that."

Chester doesn't say it but thinks, "It would be good for me. Maybe I could take an interest in Keith like I might take in a neighbor kid."

Keith adds, "And maybe when the weather warms up, I could mow your lawn."

Chester continues, "And then stay over for a steak. The grill is the only kind of cooking I do well." Chester is smiling and Keith's face is brightening. He's feeling a sense of intimacy with the last man in the world he thought possible.

Chapter 10: A Miracle

William has rolled up his shirtsleeves and scrubbed his arms and hands thoroughly with soap and hot water. Mary has washed Helen in the manner that William prescribed. There is an abundance of dry towels and extra blankets nearby.

William has given everyone their marching orders. Helen's contraction continue both in frequency and intensity. She attempts to muffle her screams into sighs but William tells her, "Cry out, woman. You're announcing a baby's coming." Helen feels new freedom to give sound to her pain. Both she and Jack are holding on tight.

The birth canal which has been widening gradually now opens enough to see the crown on the baby's head. William says, "Now Mama, just keep panting, you and the baby are going to do all the work. I'm just here to guide the baby. I'm putting my hand on the top of its head so that it doesn't come out too fast. No need for unnecessary harm to you. Now, it's coming."

Jack utters, "My God, I thought what I had already seen was the top of the head, not just the tip of it. I can't believe something this big is coming out of Helen. Oh, Helen, I'm the happiest man in the world!"

William says to Mary, "Have plenty of dry towels ready. The baby is going to be real slippery when it comes out."

As the baby progresses into the world, Jack cries out, "It's a boy! I would have been equally happy with a girl or a boy, but it's a boy!"

In an exhausted voice, Helen says, "Jack, meet little Johnny."

By now the baby has totally emerged and William holds it by his feet and rigorously dries his back with a towel. This is enough to open up the baby's lungs and a cry comes out.

Helen says, "Jack, that's your son you're hearing."

Jack lets go of Helen's hand for a moment and as she looks up she sees Jack wiping away tears. They both look into each other's eyes with a satisfying love they never thought possible.

William lays the baby on his mother's stomach head down so that the fluid leaks out of his nose. He explains, "Put some warm covers over him and his new mother, too. They both need to be kept real warm."

Jack walks over to William who is exhausted from the adrenalin of delivering the baby. Jack proclaims, "I don't have the words to thank you. I don't think such words exist." He throws his arms around William and hugs him, his head pressing into William's shoulder. It was a powerful moment for William as well, and for that moment at least, a lifetime barrier ceased to exist.

Mary exclaims, "Oh my goodness, it's after midnight! It's Christmas morning! Did anyone notice when the baby was born?"

Sandy speaks up. "I did. I looked at my watch and it was four after twelve."

After the umbilical cord is cut, William and Jack give little Johnny his first bath. Jack holds him while William quickly washes him down, and then returns him to a warm blanket.

Mary goes upstairs and removes a little yellow infant jump suit from her bottom dresser drawer. It had been intended for her little daughter who had only lived a few hours. Mary had saved it all these years as a connection to that lost child. Today she decides it's time to put that sadness behind her. She then turns to wake Joseph and says, "Joseph, your big adventure is now complete. We have a new baby boy in the house!"

Joseph leaps from bed and runs down the stairs, through the living room, and knocks on the bedroom door. He is immediately invited in by the new mother who is holding her baby son. Joseph has never seen a newborn infant before, and exclaims, "I can't believe how small his hands are! What's his name?"

Jack says, "If we were fair, we should name him William Joseph, after the two heroes of the night. But we're naming him after me. John is my real name and we're calling him Johnny."

Joseph is so pleased to be called a hero. His thoughts then return to little Johnny and says, "I've never seen such a small person!"

William adds, "He looks full size for a new baby to me. And his breathing's easy. That's the important thing."

William smells the strong fragrance of freshly brewed coffee and is drawn to the kitchen. Joseph follows him and the two of them are momentarily alone.

William says, "Joseph, I hope you realize that you are a hero."

Joseph responds, "You're the one who delivered the new baby. I'm the one who couldn't make it through the drifts."

William replies, "My friend, I don't expect you to understand this, but you opened the door for me to play the part I did."

But, in truth, Joseph does understand, even if it's on a deeper level than he can verbalize. He looks at William with a beautiful smile.

William, looking straight into Joseph's eyes, replies, "I think you do understand after all."

Chester and Keith had been introduced to Johnny before Joseph came down and were now in the living room. Sandy joins them. She has completed two assignments from Mary. The first was to cut up an old mattress cover in squares to use as diapers. The second was to gather everyone's contact information, make four additional copies, and distribute them accordingly.

Mary presents the little infant jumpsuit to Helen and Jack. She certainly doesn't mention its history; she only wants happiness for these new parents and their little boy. She can't help but notice the profound depth Helen and Jack share, and she questions if it would be possible to ignite even a portion of that kind of love into her marriage. She had always been told she was smart; she was the valedictorian of her high school class. Is she smart enough to figure out what she has to do? She knows this much: it will require a surge both of courage and vulnerability, which, she concludes, come down to the same thing. Can she do it? Time will tell.

A commotion from outside commands everyone's attention. A snowplow has arrived from the north with the phone company truck right behind it.

Once the phone is working, Mary contacts Dr. Yegerlehner in Kentland. Mary's next two calls arrange for the driveway to be cleared and to have a wrecker pull her guests' cars back onto the road.

When Dr. Yegerlehner arrives, he assesses the new baby as healthy. But he arranges for an admission to St. Elizabeth's hospital in Lafayette to be on the safe side.

Chester calls Sandy's stepdad to talk about the missing car. Larry challenges Chester, "How do I know you're who you say you are?"

Chester responds, "I'll call the Chief of Police and ask him to personally go to your house to vouch for me." Larry's response is immediate; he doesn't think that will be necessary. He'll drop the charges as long as Sandy and Keith agree not to see each other until Sandy graduates from high school.

Chester arrives at Trey's house mid-afternoon, Christmas Day.

Bernard and the older Brow children arrive home the following day.

Much to Joseph's delight, William and family stop by on their way from Louisville to their new home in Gary. They're persuaded to stay for dinner.

Epilogue

Memorial Day Weekend, 1958

Two and a half years later

Keith makes a particular effort in mowing and trimming Chester's yard. Trey and family are due. Keith will also help with the grilling, a skill Chester has taught him.

As proposed, Helen tutored Keith for his GED. It has been a rough go; Keith failed his first two attempts. The Coopers and Chester kept convincing him that he could do it, and he finally did. Not only that, he has an interview next week with Jack's brother. The fix is in.

Little Johnny looks more like his mom than his dad. At two and a half, he's a handful, in perpetual motion and talking up a storm. He realized early on that his dazzling smile could get him much of what he wants. What he doesn't comprehend is how eager his parents are to be pushovers.

Jack is still on top of the advertising game but he's no longer as driven. Last year, he did manage to land Gary Mercantile Bank as an account.

William and family have recently moved from their rented home to one they've purchased. The transaction was financed through Gary Mercantile Bank. Jack was involved.

Sandy's to graduate from high school in ten days. She has invited the whole Christmas Eve group. This includes someone she hasn't seen in over two years. She has plans for business classes starting in the fall.

Joseph just completed the sixth grade. He played on the basketball team this past winter. He wasn't very good. But he had already learned a valuable lesson a few Christmases ago: you can be a real hero just for trying.

Mary and Bernard are spending more time together, just the two of them. They're planning a trip to New York City the week of their 20th wedding anniversary. The idea is to retrace much of what they did on their honeymoon.

Sometimes a pivotal moment in life comes out of the blue. That happened to a group of people, Christmas Eve on Highway 41. All their lives had hit a reset button. They were different people going forward.

Acknowledgements

To my friend Bill Berens, who encouraged me to write this book. To my sister, Carolyn Benner, who served as editor. To Anji Strasburger who served as copy editor. And to Todd Hipsher, who helped me with every techy aspect of writing and publishing this book.